A paperba

NOW Y(

ALSO BY EMMA L BEAL

(1) NOW YOU SEE ME…

(2) NOW YOU DON'T

WWW.EMMALBEALAUTHOR.COM

www.emmalbealauthor.com

A Paperback Original 2024

First published in Great Britain by Emma L Beal 2024

Copyright © EmmaLBeal2024

This novel is a work of fiction.
The names, characters and incidents portrayed in it are the work of the author's imagination. Any resemblance to actual persons, living or dead, is entirely coincidental.

Emma L Beal has asserted her right to be identified as the author of this work in accordance with the Copyright, Designs and Patents Act 1988.

All rights reserved. No part of this publication may be reproduced, stored in a retrieval system, or transmitted in any form or by any means, electrical, mechanical, photocopying, recording or otherwise without the prior permission of the copyright owner.

Invictus

Out of the night that covers me,

Black as the pit from pole to pole,

I thank whatever gods may be

For my unconquerable soul.

In the fell clutch of circumstance

I have not winced nor cried aloud.

Under the bludgeonings of chance

My head is bloody, but unbowed …

William Ernest Henley

THE SWEETEST SMILES HIDE THE DARKEST SECRETS.

NOW YOU DON'T

Emma L Beal

One

My home.
My sanctuary.

Everything in here is tainted.
How could I now be free, only to feel trapped once more by such a sense of desolation?
Eric isn't here, and yet, I feel him all around me.

I met Eric Sawyer in May 2019 – a chance meeting really as I hadn't intended to go out that evening. I had sworn off men forever, but, Heidi, my best friend, persuaded me to slip on my best *catch-a-fella* outfit and head to *The Dirty Rabbit* for a few cheeky drinks, and meet him I did.
Do I have wonderful memories of that first encounter?
  No.
I don't have any wonderful memories of the man that would quickly become my husband, because he's tainted them all with his violence and his hatred. Anything sweet at the start of our relationship quickly spoiled. Everything that I stupidly perceived to be happiness suddenly turned

sour and went bad.

Eric was bad.

My friends warned me about him, begged me to leave, they tried to save me, they really did. But I was stupid, I believed he loved me. I was wrong and they, unfortunately, were right.

Eric's violence in our marriage escalated to such extreme levels that I knew one day he would kill me.
Everything that I did was wrong. The way I dressed, the way I behaved, the way I prepared his coffee or shut the blinds, absolutely every little thing, no matter how small, how insignificant, was wrong. And for those errors, I was punished.

Would our marriage have survived, and been somewhat normal if I'd watched my tone of voice? Agreed with everything he said and did? If I'd initiated sex more - despite my revulsion to have his hands anywhere near me? Would it have been better if I had been the *perfect* wife? Would it?
No! I could have been the epitome of perfection and it still wouldn't have been enough.

Looking back over the years that have passed with my rose-tinted glasses long removed, I can see now what my friends saw. I can admit that the way he treated me was wrong. But back then I would not have heard a bad word said about him. How stupid I was. How wrapped up in the fantasy that I wanted so desperately.

I do see it now.

I knew after the car accident that left me wheelchair-bound that I needed to escape, so I plotted in secret. I had learnt to walk again. I had such an overwhelming desire to live that even the thought of being caught fleeing would not deter me from trying. And I *had* beaten him. Despite him telling me over and over that I belonged to him, that I could never leave. I had. I had dragged my broken body through Whitby and I had escaped.

Heidi and Gordon had been my lifeline following my escape. Heidi, because she's my best friend and will always have my back, and Gordon, Heidi's brother – well, he was my saviour and I will never be able to repay him for what he did to help me.

Of course, my futile attempts at a new life in Bardsey, with a shiny new name were to be short-lived. I knew he wouldn't let me be. I knew that he would use all of his resources to find me. And that's exactly what he did.

After only three (of the best) years, he tracked me down, and the freedom that I so desperately cherished was once again snatched from me in the cruelest of ways.

There was a new man in my life by that point. A man that I had ever so slightly fallen for. Jake was the polar opposite of Eric (or so I had believed), and Eric in a jealous rage had beaten him almost to a pulp. He told me that I was never to see him again.

Of course, in the way that things always went with Eric, the situation escalated quickly. Despite once again being held captive in my own home, despite being broken and humiliated, I had beaten him at his own game once more and fled into the night with a rather confused and angry Jake. However, our bliss was once again shattered by Eric's arrival at Jake's parents' summer house. Eric would just not let me be free. He didn't know how to let go of his *possession.*

That night ended badly.

Eric was dead. Murdered by Jake.

Jake was dead. Murdered by me.

Less than one week ago Jake beat my husband to death with a rock, and between us, we dropped his dead body into a disused well.

That same night I killed Jake. It wasn't an accident; it was very much intentional. I needed to be free, I wanted to go home and he was hindering my new life. I truly had no choice.

If you could only comprehend what I have suffered, if you could only feel for one brief moment a third of what I have endured, you would have done the same.

Wouldn't you?

Eric and I never had the perfect marriage, it wasn't ever the fairy tale that I had hoped for, but for two men to now be dead because of me is something that I need to learn to live with. It's something that I need to accept. Eric was evil and he didn't deserve to live. But Jake?

Poor Jake was just weak. If I could have trusted him, if I could have had faith, just a tiny amount of faith, that he wouldn't jeopardise my freedom, then he would still be alive today. But I had no faith and I could not risk him confessing to what we had done.

I just wanted to go home.

My husband was evil and now he's dead.
I may not have delivered that fatal last blow, but I wish I had.

Two

Three days have passed since I left Bardsey.

Three days since I dragged Jake's lifeless body through the mud and the rain and dumped his corpse into the disused well at his family's summer house, alongside the dead body of my abusive husband Eric.

Three days since I scrubbed that house of all trace of me. I cleaned away the broken vase that I beat Eric with, scooped up what remained of my beautiful hair, tidied the bedroom, and washed the sheets, I scrubbed until blisters formed on my hands and then and only then did I allow myself a moment to just sit in silence, to just breathe.

Three days of wondering if I was doing the right thing. Should I confess, hand myself into the police and own up to my part in the death of these men?
Three days of convincing myself that I did the right thing. The only thing that I could do.

Three days since I packed what few belongings I had and made my way back home, back to Whitby.
And now, here I am, surrounded by the walls that were my sanctuary for the longest time, a sanctuary that quickly

became a prison. A prison that I had to fight to break free from.

I met Eric in May 2019 and finally escaped his evil clutches in October 2022 – now, December 2025, I cannot at all comprehend how I have survived the past six years. How I can be back here where it all started. Changed and yet still somehow standing.

I had been scared and nervous as I approached the door that I fled from. Not because I feared a surprise, I of all people knew that Eric was absolutely not waiting to ambush me. But, because of all the memories that would come flooding back in an overwhelming avalanche of distress the moment I saw inside again. I was not wrong.

Everything is just how I left it.

The plant pot by the front door where I would hide the books that Eric forbade me to read. The Tampax box in the bathroom where I hid the pill from Eric is still undiscovered. The cans in the cupboard are still lined up, the clothes in the wardrobe are still ordered by colour and the place is immaculate. As I knew it would be.

Eric would never have had it any other way.

However, the rooms, no matter how tidy, and how organised, still for me, harbour the darkest of memories.

The kitchen where he first raised his fist to me because

I dared to mock his OCD, it had been a joke and yet that moment had set so many other things in motion.

The table where he threw coffee in my face, the floor where he beat me as though I were nothing. The bedroom, oh god, the bedroom. His abuse, his relentless sexual assaults, the way he threatened to kick the bathroom door down as I hid, terrified and alone. The horrors that these walls have seen and heard cannot accurately be put into words.

How can I bear to be back here?

How can I step through the front door and hope to try and live here again?

Because I have nothing else. That's how.

Pushing open the door to the spare bedroom, I gasp as I see the wheelchair that I had needed during my convalescence, sitting proudly in the centre of the room. It now has ankle and wrist restraints, proving in the simplest of visual ways that Eric evidently had plans for my return, and they most certainly included blocking any future escape attempts.

If I weren't already convinced that his death was the best outcome for that madman, then I sure do now. Can you just imagine what my life would have been like had I returned with him?

The past would seem like a walk in the park.

Nobody knows that I am back. My best friend Heidi should have been the first person that I told, she has, after all, been there for me every step of the way. But to tell her that I am home would warrant an explanation of how that is even possible. She would ask about Eric, and even though I know that she would understand eventually, I just do not have it in me at this time to tell her what happened three nights ago. I can scarcely believe it myself.

I also know that I need to see my parents, who again, will ask after Eric.

So many questions and so few answers.

I just need time. I just need to be alone for a little while. To comprehend all that has happened. To get my story straight. Because even if I do tell my friends and my parents, I can never ever tell anyone else.

All they will see is a murderer.

They will not see a survivor.

I'll be dragged through the courts; the newspapers will have a field day and some lucky reporter will finally get his or her 'big break'.

My family and friends will be hounded, and every post I've ever made, shared, or liked on social media will be scrutinised!

Did anyone see this coming?

What's the real truth of Jade Locke – Was she the victim or the instigator?

Is there any actual evidence that I was a beaten wife? Other than the testimonies of my friends, Heidi especially, there will be nothing. Not one tangible scrap of proof that I was indeed the victim.

And then will come the ultimate finale, after being grilled for hours in the police station in a TV-esque good cop, bad cop routine, I will finally cave and admit to everything, and that is when they will find the bodies!

Eric's head smashed in, Jake's throat slashed open, a post-mortem will reveal it all, and I will be branded a ruthless killer. A maniac on a killing spree. A man-hater.

So, no one can ever know outside of those that I truly trust. This secret must remain watertight.

But, can secrets like this really stay secrets forever?

The first thing that I must do now that I am back is clear out all evidence of Eric. I do not want one single trace of that man left in my life, my home. I cannot live with him around me. His stuff judging me, reminding me of what I have done. I know that I can't just dump all of his belongings at the nearest tip, that would definitely look suspicious, and the curtain-twitching neighbours would have a field day wondering and gossiping about what I'm doing. I do have to wonder if they knew, the neighbours. Did they hear me scream? Did they hear me in pain and do nothing to help me? I only ask because I can hear them sometimes. Their TV, their heated conversations, so it stands to reason does it not that they would also have heard me?

What would I have done if I were on their side of the wall? I like to think that I would have helped, but I don't know. I just don't know.

In these situations people are scared, aren't they?

There is always a big part of them that wants to help, but it's always overshadowed by the fear of being told to go away, it's none of their business, interfering busybody. Or worse, being dragged unwillingly into the drama. So they pretend not to hear, they reason away what could be happening next door. Simple domestic, all couples argue, over emotional wife, she's so melodramatic, it'll blow over.

I can't honestly say that before all of this happened to me I wouldn't have done the same.

I'm sure I would have.

Maybe I can't brazenly drag Eric's belongings down

the path in view of those very neighbours, but, I can bag them up and shove them out of sight. I might then if asked, be able to say that he left me. He cleared out his belongings and vanished into the night. I could say that I came home to try and resolve things, to ask for an amicable divorce, to ask him politely to leave, but he's beaten me to it.

Would anyone believe that of Eric Sawyer?

The big man, the business owner, the charmer?... Would they?

Again, so many questions and not nearly enough answers. But if I am to stay here, to try and rebuild my life, then I need to do it without constant reminders of him. Of course, I can't rip out the kitchen, the shower, and the bedroom. But I can get a new bed, throw out that sinister-looking wheelchair, and bag up his clothes, toiletries, and books. Everything that is Eric's can be hidden away. Just as I must do with this secret.

Grabbing a handful of bin bags I begin to ram Eric's shirts and suits inside, revelling in the utter carnage that I am creating. His precious colour-coordinated wardrobe is now a jumble of coat hangers swinging freely and unprohibited. His shoes are next, then his ties, socks, underwear, and casual weekend clothes. Whatever has touched that man is heading for the gloomy depths of my bin bag, where it shall never again see the light of day.

Moving on to the bathroom I feel empowered as I gather up all of his aftershaves, deodorants and shaving balms and fling them into the bag with careless abandon. With each item I dispose of, I feel his presence weakening. I feel his emotional hold over me losing its grip, it's intoxicating.

Next are the cupboards. I won't throw away the food, that would be pointless and wasteful, but I'll be damned if I'll allow them to stay in the perfectly organised way that they are. So, grabbing tins haphazardly I begin to rearrange them, not in any particular order, sort of like a reverse version of Tetris, only with beans and soups.

Satisfied only when the cans are not in any order whatsoever, I make my way back into the bedroom and rummage through my drawers until I find the red lingerie set that he would force me to wear. And taking the very scissors that Eric sheared my hair with I begin to chop up the lacy, frilly, disgusting bra and knickers until they lay scattered on the floor like red confetti.

I strip the bed, throw a blanket over the wheelchair, shove the bags under the spare room bed, and scrub the house, every inch of it until I am one hundred per cent certain that all traces of that monster have been eradicated.

I am exhausted.

Mentally, physically, and emotionally.

I didn't expect it to be easy when I returned home. I knew that I would have a lot to deal with in terms of Eric's personal items and cleaning the house to wash away his presence. I even knew that the memories would be a challenge to deal with, but I hadn't appreciated at all just how gruelling it would be on my body and mind.

Yes, it has been invigorating to bag up his life, to remove him from my immediate line of sight. But, also it's been hard. It's just been so bloody hard.

He's gone forever and yet everything that I have endured over the years feels as though it only happened yesterday. I fear these demons will never leave me.

I desperately need to make an appointment to see Stella, my therapist in Harrogate. Of course, I cannot tell her what I've done. I don't know much about doctor / patient confidentiality, and I'm not prepared to take the risk of her contacting the police. But I do need to speak to her. Despite having only that one initial session with her, I knew even then that she would be able to help me. And even though things have escalated, things that I cannot tell her about, I still think she can help me to work through my past, help me to find a way to move on and live with all that has happened. I need to be able to do that.

Eric is gone.

Jake is gone.

But I am still very much here and I want to live a normal life. Well, as normal as normal can be in these circumstances.

It's late now. I have tried to keep myself busy, and I have put off the inevitable – sleeping in *that* bed. But I am tired. I am so very tired.

And he is gone.

He is gone.

Three

'Wakey, wakey, Jadey.'

Rough, calloused hands gripped loosely around my throat rouse me from my sleep as I struggle to comprehend what is happening.

'Hello, *wife*.' Eric snarls, as his face slowly comes into focus in the gloom. 'Did you miss me?'

I'm frozen, just for a moment as the fog of sleep begins to clear, and then I scream. Scrambling from beneath him I throw myself from the bed and bolt for the door, as his laughter follows me out into the living room.

How is this possible?

How is he here?

'Ah, c'mon Jadey, have you nothing to say? No kiss for your husband?'

'What…?'

'What's that?' he laughs. 'What am I doing here? Oh, Jade.' He snarls as he moves slowly towards me, 'You didn't think one little well would stop me, did you? I must admit, I was somewhat surprised when that James fella came tumbling in after me. Who knew you had it in you?

My wife. The killer.'

'His name was JAKE!' I scream as I run from him once more, only to be stopped in my tracks by the sight of the wheelchair once again sitting proudly in the centre of the spare bedroom.

'You found my gift I see. Why don't you give it a try, and see what you think.'

'I'm not getting in *that thing*.' I spit. 'You won't get away with this, not again.'

'*I* won't get away with it? You should be more concerned for yourself, after all, you murdered one man and tried to murder your husband. What exactly do *I* need to worry about?'

'Everything you did to me! You should be dead! You are supposed to be dead!' I sob.

'And yet I'm not.' He smirks. 'Get in the chair. I'm not taking any more chances with you.'

'I will not.' I cry, as I try again to move away from him. This man should be rotting in a well. This man should have been out of my life forever. How the hell is he back? I saw Jake with my own eyes cave his head in, there was blood, so much blood. And yet here he stands, as immaculate as always. How did he get out of that well?

'You are dead!' I yell into his perfectly handsome face. A

face that shows no signs at all of all that we did to him. It's been less than a week – there would be something. Nobody heals that fast!

This isn't real.

This isn't real.

And yet, it feels oh so very real to me.

'You tried to kill me, *wife*! You tried and you failed. You ran from me. I found you. Did you honestly think I would let you leave? That I would let you do this to *me*?'

'How did you get out of that well?' I whimper, 'how?'

'That's for me to know.' He smirks, as he gets ever closer to me.

'You are dead.' I cry. 'You are dead!'

'Get in the chair, Jade!'

'No!'

The slap comes out of nowhere, as his palm connects sharply with the side of my face, throwing me backwards, and as my ears begin to ring, I scream. He has me again and I'm powerless once more to stop him. I once again feel a familiar darkness descending.

RING!

RING!

RING!

Waking with a start, I leap from the bed. My heart

pounding, and my hands shaking. Where is he?

The ringing continues, piercing my brain with its incessant trill as I run from room to room.

He is not here.

His belongings are still hidden beneath the bed, the wheelchair is still covered with the blanket, and the doors and windows are locked – he is most definitely not here. Sobbing with relief I realise that Eric is not back.

It was all a horrid nightmare.

And yet, the ringing continues.

Rubbing my eyes and trying my hardest to drag myself into the here and now, I realise that the ringing is my mobile phone. Rummaging through my handbag I snatch up the offensive thing that is causing me to develop a headache and bark into the handset.

'What?!'

'Jade? Jade is that you?'

'Heidi?'

'Jade, where the hell are you?' she asks, evidently concerned.

'Erm… at home.' I squeak, 'I'm at home?'

'Are you asking me or telling me.' She laughs. 'Want to maybe answer the bloody door, it's freezing, and I'm carrying what can only be described as a baby elephant,

Christ knows what Gordon has bought you for Christmas but it weighs a bloody tonne!'

'You're here?' I mumble, confused.

'Yes.' She sighs, impatiently. 'And as cute as Bardsey is, your neighbours are giving me some right funny looks. So can you let me in before they call the cops?'

'You're in Bardsey?'

'Jesus Jade, have you had a bump on the head? Yes, I'm outside, right now, and freezing my tits off I might add. You want to let me in?'

'But, but... I'm not there.'

'What do you mean you're not here? You just said that you're at home? Am I missing something?'

'I'm... well the thing is... I'm...'

'Spit it out! Bloody hell, it's like pulling teeth with you. Where are you, Jade?'

'Whitby.' I mumble, nervously, 'I'm in Whitby.'

It doesn't take long for Heidi to jump in her car, bomb it up the motorway and begin pounding on my door. I dread to think how fast she's driven and how many laws she's broken, but that's Heidi for you, she doesn't worry about silly little things like the law when her friends need her. And now as I open the door full of trepidation, unsure how

I can even begin to explain the mess that I find myself in, I am almost thrown to the floor as she rushes past me, as though she is completely oblivious to my presence, her shoulders set in angry defiance.

'Eric!' She yells as she runs from room to room, slamming doors in her wake, 'Eric you piece of shit, get out here right now!'

'Heidi, he's…'

'Eric!' Turning to face me, she looks confused and determined all at once, 'Right, so he's out, yeah? Let's get your shit packed and get the hell out of here before he comes back.'

'He's not…'

As though suddenly realising that something is amiss she strides back towards me and touches my head, 'Did he do this again?' she cries painfully. 'Again!'

'I…'

'I'll kill him!' she howls as she marches once more into my bedroom, 'Your suitcase in here?' Flinging open my suitcase she starts to throw clothes, underwear, and shoes haphazardly into it. 'You need anything else?' Her head pokes around the door, 'think quick because we're not coming back.'

'I don't…'

Ignoring me once more she flounces from my bedroom into the spare bedroom, and before I can stop her she yanks the blanket from the wheelchair and I hear her sob. 'Oh, Jesus. I'll kill him! What is this Jade? What the hell is this? Did he put you in this, this, *thing*?!'

'He's gone, Heidi.' I finally blurt out. 'He's gone.'

'He wants to make sure he stays gone as well, the bastard!' She fumes as she covers the wheelchair once more. 'I am so sorry that I did not know.' She weeps. 'What the hell kind of friend am I? You must hate me, you must! I should have…'

'Stop. This isn't your fault, it isn't my fault, it's just, I don't know, it's just something that happened and now it won't ever again.'

'I knew Jade, I knew he was wrong, I should have been more forceful, I should have made you listen...'

'You and I both know that I wouldn't have. You tried; you begged me to leave him…'

'I should have *made* you leave him; I should have contacted one of Ethan's old crew, they'd have gotten rid of him!'

'No.' I snap. 'No! You never ever contact anyone to do with that piece of shit!'

I know that's rich coming from me. I am the last person

who should be telling another woman to stay away from her crazy ex, but Ethan was a nasty piece of work, and he's in prison paying for that behaviour, Ethan is not a person to be trifled with, and even if he could have *gotten rid* of Eric, the emotional toll on Heidi would never have been worth that question being asked.

'We should get going, okay. You can stay with me, we'll get you divorced from this arsehole, sell this place if you want to, but we need to go, now.'

'We don't.' I sigh. 'We don't need to go anywhere, not anymore.'

'I know you're scared, I do, but…'

'He's dead.' I whisper. 'Eric is dead.'

Four

'**D**ead?' The silence is palpable as Heidi momentarily stops flinging clothes into my suitcase, 'Okay.' She nods, 'Dead. I get it. Metaphorically speaking he *is* dead, to *you*. It's understandable that you feel that way, of course it is, but dead *metaphorically* and dead *really* are two very different things Jade, and seeing as though we are working on the metaphorical basis here we still need to get our arses into gear and get moving.'

I don't know why I mentioned it, it was like my brain was screaming at me to shut the hell up but my lips weren't listening.

Nobody was ever supposed to know.

Nobody!

'Jade? You had some kind of glitch over there?'

'Sorry, what?' I mumble as I give my head a shake. 'Did you say something?'

'Erm, yeah.' She laughs, 'I said that you are a total weirdo so it's a good job I love you. C'mon, grab your handbag and let's get the hell out of here. If we time it right we can get to *The Dirty Rabbit* before it gets super busy.'

'I can't, I need to...'

'No. No, you're right. A piss-up is not what you need. What you need is a big fat cheesy pizza and some trashy shit on Netflix, and lucky for you I can provide both.' She grins.

'That does sound good.' I smile in spite of myself, 'but I need to tell you something first, okay. Something serious, something that might mean you never want to eat pizza and watch Netflix with me ever again. So...'

'Okay.' She mumbles as she drops down onto my bed, 'I very much doubt anything would make that happen, but I'm here for you, no matter what.'

Pushing aside my suitcase I join Heidi on the bed, not at all sure how I can even begin to put this into words. In just a few short sentences I could lose my best friend. I could lose everything. But how can I move forward, how can I let her take me in, feed me, and love me when I am keeping something from her that could intrinsically change her life should this ever be made public.

She needs to know. I cannot lie to her.

With a deep breath, I take her hands in mine and jump right in with both feet and no idea where I am going to land and who is going to catch me.

'Eric is dead, Heidi. Not metaphorically. But really. He

is really, very much in the literal sense, dead.'

'Okay. So what happened? Has there been an accident? Not that I'm disappointed, I just hope that it was awful and bloody painful. Did you push him down the stairs? Accidentally on purpose behead him with a snow shovel? Whatever.' She shrugs, 'I'll be your alibi. Seriously though, why didn't you call me, I'd have come and picked you up. You know I'd have totally helped you hide the body.' She giggles.

As Heidi's questions tumble haphazardly over one another I can't help but smile. Even in the confusion and the unknown she still has my back, despite being utterly oblivious to just how close to the truth she really is.

'He's dead and everything is just a big fat mess. I don't know what I'm going to do.'

'What *you're* going to do? What the hell has happened Jade? How *exactly* did he die?'

'I don't even know where to begin answering that question. Maybe I shouldn't have said anything, just forget…'

'Woah, woah, woah! You can't just drop that on me and then go all radio silence! Look…' She smiles as she wriggles next to me on the bed and wraps her arm around my shoulders, '…it can't be *that* bad – so spit it out.'

'Okay. But please know that I will totally understand if you don't want anything to do with me once I've told you. I won't try to stop you if you want to leave and I won't…'

'Jade! Stop! That is not going to happen, okay?'

Nodding but still unsure I slowly begin to explain all that transpired three days ago. 'Eric found me. I always knew that he would, as if I could ever be allowed to be free. What a stupid dream that was. He'd been watching me for a while, saw me with Jake, my friends, my new life and all he could think about was destroying everything that I'd built for myself, and it wasn't even much, you know. Just a simple, happy life. I didn't have anything. I didn't have you, my mum and dad, the girls, I had nothing. But I was happy, and that was too much for him – I wasn't under his control.

So, he beat Jake, locked me in the house, and chopped off my hair – again! It was like everything that I'd escaped from, everything that I'd suffered was being unleashed upon me again, but tenfold!

I don't know how I got out of that house Heidi, but I did, and I ran. Jake helped me and we hid away at his parents' summer house, I thought finally, someplace he would never find me, someplace that he could never know about. But he did know – he knew everything, he was always five steps ahead – he always was.

Anyway, he followed us there, he and Jake fought and Eris was killed. Just like that. Gone.'

'Jesus Jade! But you didn't kill him – I don't see what you're so worried about? Surely the police will...'

'We never called the police.' I sob, 'Heidi, we dragged his body through the woods and dumped it in a well! In a bloody well!'

Standing now, Heidi begins to pace the room. 'Okay, so, you know I'm not his number one fan, I'm not even remotely sorry that he's dead – but Jade, why would you do that? Why not just call the police, tell them what happened?'

'Because Jake said that I would be blamed for his murder.'

'What?! Get him on the phone right now, I am not having this.'

'I can't.'

'Sure you can, pass me the phone.'

'I can't Heidi, because he's dead too!'

'Jade! Fuck! What the hell happened? How is he dead too?'

Unable to look my best friend in the eyes, I take a deep steadying breath and mutter the words that I have been dreading. Words that I swore I would never speak. 'He's dead because I killed him. I killed him, Heidi! I killed him! I killed him! I killed him…' I scream, unable to stop now, unable to deal with what I have done.

Grabbing me by the shoulders, Heidi pulls me to her and rocks me back and forth, 'Okay, okay, it's all going to be okay. Shush, shush, I'm here, I've got you. I've always got you.'

'I'm a murderer.' I sob, 'I'm going to spend my life in prison. I deserve to. I should hand myself in, confess, I should…'

'You should take a moment and breathe. I just need time to think.'

'What is there to think about? I killed him, Heidi.'

'What exactly happened to Jake?'

'He was going to jeopardise everything. I knew he'd never be able to keep quiet, he certainly wasn't happy that I was coming back home to Whitby. I just knew that he would crack and I couldn't risk that. I just wanted to come home!'

'I know you did honey. I know. So what did you do?'

'I stabbed him.' I whisper, 'I stabbed him while he was in the shower.'

'And where is Jake now?' she asks, her voice trembling.

'He's…' I sniff, 'he's…'

'Yeah?'

'He's in the well with Eric!'

'Oh, Jesus Christ! Jesus, Jade! You dragged his dead body through the woods, on your own?'

'I had no choice.'

'You did have a choice!' She thunders, 'You call your best friend and you share the load! I'd have helped you Jade; I'd have done anything to help you! Why in God's name would you suffer this alone? Why?!'

'I couldn't call you up! What would I have said, *Oh hey Heids, I just killed a guy, wanna help me hide his bloody corpse*?!'

'Yeah. That's exactly what you should have said!'

'You're insane!'

'And dumping two dead men in a well isn't?'

'I couldn't drag you into that. I couldn't have put you in that position. I just couldn't.'

'If you'd put me in that position when you met Eric then this wouldn't be happening!'

I know as soon as she's spoken the words that she instantly regrets them. But she's right. Of course she is.

'Jade.' She pleads, 'I am so sorry, I did not mean that.'

'Sure you did.' I smile, sadly. 'And you're right to say it because it's true. I didn't listen to you, not once. You tried to warn me Heidi, and I should have known, after everything that you went through with Ethan, I should have known that you saw something that I just plain refused to see. So you are right to say it.'

'No, I'm not. It was hurtful and mean, and I'm sorry. I just wish that I'd known what was truly happening – what that arsehole was doing to you! Just like I wish that I'd known about this. You need to promise me that from now on you won't keep anything from me. You so much as sneeze then I want to know that a cold is on the way, got it?'

'It's not going to matter much now is it, when I'm in prison, eating gruel and lifting weights!'

'Lifting weights? I think that might be the least of your problems – it's the orange jumpsuits - totally not your colour by the way, and the butch birds that'll make you their bitch that you want to be concerned about.' She laughs, nudging me until I laugh too. 'Oh, and the shared toilets – you are going to hate that!'

'What am I going to do? How can I avoid this? Someone will report them missing at some point and the first place the police will come is here.'

'Then we need a plan, and that plan is going to need wine and pizza.'

'You don't have to help me. I'll understand if you want to

bail, forget you even know me...'

'You really are dumb! I'm not going anywhere, you're my best friend, my sister and I love you. So, you order the pizza, I'll pop out and grab two, hmmm, four, bottles of wine, and we will make a plan that the *A-Team* would envy.'

Pulling her into a hug, I kiss her cheek and thank her for everything. For always being there for me and most of all for not judging me.

'Not judging you?' She hollers. 'Just you wait 'til the wine kicks in!'

Three bottles of *Nisa's* finest plonk in, we have no solid idea at all of what we are going to do, but we can guarantee a healthy hangover in the morning, with a side of nausea to finish it off.

Heidi thinks the best way to deal with this is just to ignore it. Feign ignorance. *'Well, I just assumed that Eric had left me. I came back to an empty house and I'm just as shocked as everyone else. As for Jake, well, we broke up, I haven't seen or heard from him since I left Bardsey.'*

It isn't much of a plan. It's not a plan at all really. It's exactly what I planned to do anyway – well, it would have been had I not opened my big mouth and spilt out my guts to Heidi the second I saw her. But, knowing that I have her on my side, knowing that I have someone I can talk to about all of this is somewhat reassuring. All I need to do now is convince the rest of the world.

I need to act normal.

I need to remain calm.

I need to deny everything.

I think this may be easier said than done. But she is right. If I admit this, if I confess, then everything that I have fought for, everything that I have done will have been for nothing. All I will see for those wretched six years will be my freedom taken from me once more.

I will not allow that to happen.

Not again.

Five

Mum and dad's house is decked up like Santa's Grotto and to say that they are well into the Christmas spirit would be a major understatement. Not satisfied with having the best garden in Robin Hoods Bay, my mum also likes to outshine the neighbours with her fabulous Christmas lights – honestly, my poor dad puts up with a lot.

Standing outside now, watching the fairy lights twinkle and the huge inflatable snowman rocking gently in the breeze, I can't help but feel emotional. I didn't ever dare believe that I would be back here, that I could freely walk into my parents' home without Eric's shadow looming over me. I don't know what I am going to tell them. I have nothing planned because everything I planned to say just sounded ridiculous. I will think of something, but it most certainly will not be the truth.

A big part of me thinks that I should prepare them, that I should confess, just in case the worst does happen and I am eventually caught, the bodies are found and I am imprisoned, but Heidi disagrees and says that we will cross that bridge if we ever come to it.

Is it the right decision?

Well, I'm hardly the best person to judge that, am I?

They don't know that I'm back in Whitby, and I am aware that questions will be asked. They will want to know where Eric is, and if our marriage is truly over. I had of course told them somewhat briefly that I had left Eric when I moved to Bardsey, so it shouldn't be too much of a shock that he's 'upped and gone' – it's just the rest of the story that must remain a secret, even to them.

Taking one final deep breath, I push open the front door and shout out a hearty hello that is merry enough not to raise suspicion, and as mum appears in the doorway, her apron covered in goodness knows what and flour sprinkles on her cheeks, I can't help but smile.

My mum, the epitome of what home is.

'Jade?' she screeches as she rushes towards me, 'Jade, is that really you?' Flinging her arms around me, she holds me close and I don't care that I'm now also covered in flour, I don't care, because I'm home. 'George!' she bellows, 'George, you'll never guess who's here! George!' Running her hands through my hair she frowns. 'You here alone?'

'I am.' I smile, 'it's just me.'

'Right, well, that's good. I don't think your father would have allowed that... that... well... *him* into the house.'

'You don't have to worry about that mum – he's gone.'

'He's moved out? We did wonder what would happen to your house with you gone. Dad was going to hire somebody to have him evicted.'

'That would have been a sight to see.' I chuckle, 'but yeah, he's definitely no longer in the house and won't be coming back.'

'If you need the money for a divorce...'

'Thanks, mum, but I've got it covered.'

'And what about you?' she sniffs, touching my hair again, 'how are you, really?'

'I'm okay mum.' I smile as brightly as I can. 'For the first time in a long time, I'm okay.'

'You know it's okay not to be okay, don't you?'

I want to laugh because clearly, mum has been Googling motivational quotes again, but I don't, because she's right. It is okay not to be okay.

'I know mum. But I am, truly, I am. I'm just glad to be home. Heidi has been wonderful as always; she's really helping me get back on my feet.'

'She's a good friend that one. She's been texting me every day since you've been gone. And as lovely as that's been, it's not nearly as great as having you home.'

'Jade?' As dad shuffles into the hallway I can't help but notice the anger that flashes in his eyes as he sees me for the first time in so long. I know that he knows why I ran from my marriage, he isn't stupid. I also know that he will never ask me about it, he will just know, silently and angrily. 'You look well.' He lies.

'Erm, thanks.'

'Cup of tea lovey?' mum asks, breaking the awkwardness of the moment – because tea fixes everything – and as we follow her into the kitchen, dad takes my hand and gives it a little squeeze. Yes, he knows.

Settled at the dining table with a hot cup of tea and a slice of Christmas cake in front of me, I take a moment to just count my blessings, and really acknowledge and appreciate where I am.

I made it.

Somehow all of those years of terror, living on a knife's edge have all accumulated into this moment. A moment that I never thought I would have again. It's magical.

I am free now, and I fought damn hard for this. So, no matter what has happened or what is yet to come, I am going to live my life and I am going to focus on myself. What will be will be. If it catches up with me then so be it.

But now, this moment? This is all mine.

'What are your plans now you're back?' Dad questions, interrupting my thoughts.

'Well, I definitely need to get a new job. Gordon didn't charge me any rent for that house in Bardsey, but gran's inheritance isn't going to last forever, so I need to get some cash coming in – even if it's just to build up my savings again. I need to get a new car, reconnect with my friends, and put my home back in order. A lot.' I laugh. 'I have a lot of plans.'

'You don't need to rush into any of those things though.' Dad frowns. 'You don't want to be burning yourself out. If you need some money…'

'Thanks, dad, but I'm okay. I'm not totally broke. I'm looking forward to working again actually, being back in the community. I was thinking of asking Mr. Timmons if he'd let me have my old job back at the souvenir shop, but I think I might have burnt my bridges there.'

'Are you kidding?' he scoffs, 'I was only speaking to Mr Timmons yesterday when I went in for the papers, he was asking after you – he always does.'

'Yeah? Maybe I'll give him a call tomorrow.'

'Good girl.' He smiles. 'Now as for the car, you can take your mums' if you want to – she doesn't use it these days.'

'I couldn't do that.' I argue. 'Mum, what if you need it?'

'I don't dear. I haven't driven in a long time. To tell you the truth, I don't really like it.'

'What? The car?'

'Driving Jade. I don't like driving. Too many idiots on the road. And well, after that awful accident you were in, it's put me right off.'

'Aww mum, you can't stop driving because I was stupid.'

Mum is of course referring to that cold December day back in two thousand twenty-one when Eric had permitted me one hour to leave the house to go Christmas shopping. I had tried to hide the bruises on my face, but no matter how much makeup I applied, they would not be concealed. Heidi had spotted me whilst I was out shopping, and through embarrassment and shame at my appearance, I had run from her. She had of course given chase and in my desperation to not be seen I had run straight into the path of an unsuspecting car driver.

I had been hospitalised after that and placed into an induced coma for four months as my body healed.

Four months of not seeing Eric's face. I had dreamt the most wonderful dreams. But when I woke, there he was. My tormentor. My nemesis. And despite being wheelchair-bound for a short time, his abuse had continued. He was in fact even more deranged.

But my stupid accident should not put mum off driving. That would be yet another wasteful thing to come out of this whole shitty situation.

'Mum...'

'I'd just hate to think that I had hit somebody's child with my car.' She shudders, 'I don't think I could live with myself.'

'It was an accident...'

'No. It's settled, you take the car. I'll get the keys. Dad will give you some money for petrol.'

'That's not...'

However, mum is no longer listening, and as she wanders off in search of the car keys dad turns to me, his face serious.

'Jade.' He begins, somewhat apprehensively. 'You know I'm not one for sentimental chit-chat, but I need you to know that while I may not fully understand what happened with *him*, I do know that he hurt my little girl, possibly in ways that no father should ever hear about. And, well, I suppose what I'm trying to say is, I'm here if you need me, for anything, anything at all. All I ask is that you don't leave again. It would break our hearts to not have you near. And of course, it goes without saying that if *he* ever comes back…'

Choking back tears, I stand and hold my dad for what may be the longest time ever in our entire relationship. I hold him so tight that I know it's hurting him, but he does not grumble, because he knows that I need this just as much as he does.

'I'm so sorry.' I sob. 'So, so sorry.'

Pulling me onto his knee, he rocks me as he did so many years ago when I was a child, 'You never apologise to me, do you hear. Never. Now, wipe those tears, because there'll be hell to pay if your mother thinks I've made you cry, and I'll never hear the end of it.'

'Thanks, dad.'

'Just remember what I said.' He whispers just as mum triumphantly drops the car keys onto the table.

'So, what did I miss?' she asks, as dad winks at me.

'Nothing mum.' I smile. 'Everything is just as it should be.'

Six

Dad was right, Mr Timmons was happy to give me my old job back, in fact, he was downright ecstatic – I have a feeling that dad may have spoken with him already because he wasn't at all surprised to see me.

I'm starting back on a part-time basis, despite Mr. Timmons trying to throw hours at me. I will return full-time at some point, but for now, just a few hours a week will be perfect.

I have a lot to sort out, including making a long overdue appointment with my therapist, but for now, just for today, I want to be free to wander around Whitby, to do all of the things that I was forbidden to do for so long, and first on that list is a lemon topped ice-cream from *Trillo's*, followed closely by a walk on the beach and a paddle in the icy cold sea.

I know, I know, it's December – who eats ice cream in December? But let me just say, if you haven't experienced the sharp tang of the lemon top ice cream then you are truly missing out, and if you have, well, you know where I'm coming from.

I hope it's open, I am so behind with everything in Whitby now that I'm no longer sure what is where and what has gone, but to get to it I must walk past the *White Horse and Griffin*. Unfortunately, the streets are somewhat deserted as Whitby is no longer in peak tourist season, which leaves me unable to blend in as I would normally attempt to do with passing families or guided tours.

I know obviously that Eric is not in the pub, but, like the last time and the many times before, his friends will be – and we all know what happened the last time I encountered one of his drinking buddies on this street.

I wish that Eric hadn't claimed the *White Horse and Griffin* as his own, because it truly is exceptional. The food, the atmosphere, the history. I know that we have *The Dirty Rabbit*, our favoured bolt hole, but sometimes I wish that I could visit the *White Horse and Griffin* again.

Maybe one day, when all of this is over and life has returned to normal I will be able to do just that. Maybe with Eric gone, it won't be off-limits anymore.

I'll be passing *The Whitby Bookshop* on my way to the harbour, and as I haven't read anything good in a long time I might as well seize this opportunity to stick my head in and have a good look around. It's a nice feeling to know that I won't have to hide my books in the plant pot anymore. In fact, I'm going to order a bookcase when I get back home, a nice big one, and I am going to fill it with all of the books that I was forbidden to read. I am going to make it the focal point of my home. My bookcase. My books. My life.

Peering through the window now, I can't help the bubble of excitement and anticipation that is building inside of me. And as I chuckle, just a little, at the simplicity of this moment, at the pure delight of just looking in a shop window with no time restrictions and no fear, I don't immediately notice the shadow looming over me.

'Hello, Jade.'

I know who it is before I even look his way. I knew it would be a mistake to linger on this street, to think that I could just slot back into my life. I knew, didn't I, that it was never going to be that easy. Despite Ben being Eric's best friend we had never gelled. I had always found him to be abrasive, an irritant that gets right under your skin like the proverbial thorn in your side. When he would visit to collect Eric for the pub, I would hate how he stood too close to me, his lip curling back in a half snarl, his breath hot on my neck. Eric had never been bothered though; he hadn't cared that I had felt uncomfortable. He had just laughed along with him. Throughout my marriage, I had tried my hardest to avoid Ben. But I would know his voice anywhere.

'Ben.' I gulp as I turn to face him, wondering if I can get around him and into the shop without causing a scene. 'It's...'

'Don't say *good to see me.*' He sneers. 'We both know that's bullshit. Where is he, Jade?'

'Who?' I ask, timidly, as I once again eyeball the front door of the shop, 'where is who?'

'You know.' He smirks, 'I knew you weren't right for Eric, the moment I clapped eyes on you, I knew. I can totally understand why he had to keep you on such a short leash. Why he had no other choice but to limit your freedom. You're an embarrassment to him, do you know that? He couldn't have you running around besmirching his good name, I had an idea of course, that something was wrong, with you.'

'There's nothing wrong with me, you have no idea at all what I've been through, what *he* put me through.' I snap, as I move around him.

'Oh I do, I even suggested some of those things to him. Women like you need keeping in their place.'

'Women like *me?*! And what the hell would you know

about me?'

'I know *you've* done something to him. I don't know what and I don't know how, but I will find out.'

'This is crazy, you're as nuts as he is!'

'Funny though.' He ponders as he reaches out and pulls my scarf tighter around my neck. 'How you ran from me that day, and then, poof! You up and disappear, and then so does Eric. So, I'll ask again, where is he?'

'It was *you* that chased me? I could have been killed on that bridge.'

'Nobody made you make a jump for it, Jade. I only wanted to talk.'

Laughing, I push his hands away from my face and reach for the door handle of the shop, 'I highly doubt that's correct. Men like you don't know how to talk without using their fists, I learnt that the hard way from your *friend*!'

'Where is he?'

'I don't know! How many more times do I have to tell you!'

'I will find out Jade, you mark my words.'

'There's nothing to find out, so you'll be wasting your time.'

'Eric has never just vanished before. He's not answering

his phone or texts, not replying to emails! So you can understand my concern, I'm sure.'

'Concern?'

'Yes, Jade, concern. Eric is missing, and, well, you are his loving, faithful wife, are you not?'

'No, Ben. I'm not.' Turning from him once more I shakily push open the door to the shop and step inside, 'I don't know where he is, and if you harass me again I'll have you arrested. Stay away from me.'

'Oh, Jade.' He laughs, 'I'll be sticking to you like glue. I'll be your shadow until Eric is found. Interesting isn't it, that you haven't reported him missing?'

'There is nothing interesting about it. I left him Ben; I left your *best buddy* and I started a new life. How Eric has or hasn't dealt with that is his problem. You want to follow me? Fine. But I do not know where he is, and I don't care. Our marriage is over and has been for a long time. I would have thought as his friend you would have known that. Or do men like you only share their victories? *Oh the shame, his wife left him*! He couldn't possibly admit to that, could he!'

'He hasn't lost Jade, because he has me looking out for him, and I will get to the bottom of this.'

'You're like a broken record, you and Eric alike. I'll say it one more time, if you harass me or stalk me again, I will contact the police.'

'Shame you didn't do that when your husband went missing. There's still time though, shall we go now, together?'

'Goodbye Ben.' I smile. 'Oh, and you're right, it isn't at all good to see you.'

Entering the shop, all thoughts of my new bookcase momentarily obliterated, I make my way to the furthest corner, away from his prying eyes and just stand for a moment, digesting all that has just happened. The last thing I need is Ben looking into Eric's disappearance, and I'm fairly certain there isn't enough room in that well for another full-grown man.

Or is there?

Stifling a chuckle that I know is inappropriate considering the circumstances, I shake myself down and head for the fiction section of the shop, my lemon top ice cream all but forgotten. I need to escape my life for a while, and for that, I will need books. Lots and lots of books.

I can't concentrate.

It has nothing to do with the book that I'm trying to read

and everything to do with my encounter this morning, as Ben's words spin around and around in my mind, making it damn near impossible to focus on anything else but him.

'I will find out Jade, you mark my words.'

'I'll be sticking to you like glue. I'll be your shadow until Eric is found.'

Why can't these people just leave me alone?

I knew that Eric was close to his cronies in the pub, but I had no idea that he was close enough to them to seek out their advice on how to torture me. Just how many of his friends do I now need to worry about?

I know that I don't have any right at all to take the moral high ground here. I haven't forgotten what I've been a part of and what I've done. How could I?

But Jesus Christ, don't I deserve to have a life? Don't I at least deserve to have a moment where I can just remember what it's like to be Jade Locke?

The free woman?

The woman who had a happy life before all of this madness?

The woman who wasn't a killer?

Putting my book down with a frustrated sigh, I switch on the TV and find the local news channel.

Surely they would both have been reported missing by

now?

But there's nothing.

The news is as it always is.

Energy Crisis.

Cost of fuel.

Cost of food.

Not one single word is uttered about two men just vanishing into thin air. Not one.

How can this be?

Does nobody miss them?

Is it possible that the police do know, but they're keeping it quiet while they investigate? They could have me in their sights already and I just don't know it, yet.

Or, is it possible that they aren't missing at all and they somehow made it out of that well?

I know it's absolute nonsense. They were both dead. Very, very dead! And yet, it's the only thing that makes sense. They haven't been reported missing, because they are not in fact bloody missing!

I can understand nobody reporting Eric missing, well, apart from my new best friend, Ben. The man was a psychopath! But Jake?

Jake was liked by so many, even by me at one point. So why has his disappearing act not set things in motion that will inevitably lead to my downfall?

Because they made it out of the well, that's how!

Am I crazy?

Am I overthinking this because of the stress and worry?

Am I right?

Flicking off the TV, I pace the room, unable to sit still, unable to think of anything other than Eric and Jake climbing out of that well, bloodied and angry.

I should leave.

I should leave Whitby.

I should change my name, start a new life someplace else, forget about Jade Locke, forget about my home and my family and friends. I should turn my back on everything that I have fought to return to – because if Eric is free, then I am already in terrible danger.

He will come for me and at that point, I'll be praying that I'm arrested and charged with double murder. I'll be begging for a prison cell. I'll be pleading for a hefty sentence – because the alternative would be so much worse.

He will be so much worse.

Grabbing the remote again, I switch the TV back on. Still, there is nothing. Not a peep. Just more of the same.

Energy Crisis.

Cost of fuel.

Cost of food.

They didn't get out of that well.

They were dead Jade; I whisper to myself.

You are overreacting.

It's just your guilty conscience playing tricks on you.

THEY WERE DEAD!

Weren't they?

HORROR UNFOLDS IN SLEEPY VILLAGE AS TWO MEN ARE DISCOVERED IN A DISUSED WELL- **ALIVE!**

Dog walker, Joe Malone, 56, had set out as he does every morning for his daily dog walk and was horrified to discover two men, barely alive, screaming from the bottom of a disused well.

Mr Malone stated that this walk was not his usual route, as the land is, in fact, private property, but when his dog, Bella ran off ahead of him, he had no choice but to give chase.

It was Bella who alerted Mr Malone to the distress calls of these two terrified men, and he immediately alerted emergency services, who were quick to arrive at the scene.

It is not clear at this point how the men came to be in the well, but both appear to be responding well to treatment at Leeds General Infirmary and a police investigation is now underway.

If anybody has any information regarding the welfare or identity of these two individuals, they are urged to contact West Yorkshire Police.

Seven

I wake screaming as a cold sweat slithers across my body.

Flinging myself from the bed I run through to the lounge and turn on the TV, my heart threatening to bounce right out of my chest as I wait, for the news to tell me what I already know – Eric and Jake are alive!

Where is it?

Where is this damn news report?

Hands shaking, I surf all of the channels that are available to me, trying to find anything that corroborates the story I have just seen with my own eyes – where the hell is it?

I saw it I cry, as I sink to my knees in front of the screen. I saw it.

I know that I did.

There's nothing here! Just the same depressing shit as yesterday. Fuel, Food, Energy! Some random celebrity and her all-out war divorce! It's all just shit!

Maybe I am going crazy. Maybe I'm seeing things that just aren't there. But as heavy pounding booms through the house, I know that I am wrong. It *was* true and the police are here to hammer that confirmation home.

What do I do?

This is going to shatter my parents. My Friends. Me.

And still, the pounding continues.

I need to leave, now!

Rushing through to the bedroom I throw on yesterday's clothes and pull my suitcase down from the top of the wardrobe. I can't think. I don't know what to do.

Wait it out? Pray they'll leave?

'Jade! For the love of Christ, can you open the bloody door, it's freezing! You are so giving me a key!'

Heidi?

The person banging on my door like a lunatic is Heidi!

She must know.

She's here because she's seen the news too!

'Jade? I am going to ninja-kick this door down. Jade?'

What if she's not alone?

What if it's all a ploy to get me to open up and the police are right outside with her?

'Jade? I need to pee, can you please let me in!'

I have no choice. I don't think my best friend would do the dirty on me like this, I don't. But if she has, and the police are out there, then I guess this is it.

'Just a sec.' I shout out as cheerily as I can. 'Just getting my keys.'

'I'm peeing here, Jade! Hurry up already.'

Shakily, unlocking the door, I am ready for the handcuffs to be slapped on my wrists as I'm then escorted past my neighbours to a waiting police car. But none of that happens. Instead, I am nearly knocked off my feet as Heidi barges past me and runs for the bathroom. Something that has become a regular occurrence with her recently.

'Jesus, Jade, that was a close call.'

She is alone.

No police. No Handcuffs. No waiting police car.

What the hell is going on?

Shutting the door, I hear Heidi flush the toilet and then wash her hands. There is no sense of urgency now at all. And as she saunters back into the living room she laughs.

'Bloody hell. I had to do a little dance before I could even get my pants down. Morning Bestie.' She grins.

'What are you doing here? What time is it?'

'I know, I know, it's super early, but I wanted to see how you were doing, and I couldn't sleep last night, so I…'

'You've seen it too, haven't you?' I sigh as I sink down onto the sofa. 'It's over.'

'What's over? I'm confused.'

'My life, Heidi! My life is over! Haven't you seen the news? They're not dead! They got out of the bloody well!'

'Okay, okay, slow down. What news report is this?' She asks as she picks up the remote and begins to click through the channels, 'There's nothing here, just the normal doom and gloom.'

'Two men found in disused well! I saw it Heidi, I did.'

Turning the TV off she slides next to me on the sofa. 'When did you see it?'

'I don't know.' I shrug. 'I just woke up this morning and knew I'd seen it. Two men found in disused well!'

'You woke up? Do you think maybe it was a bad dream?'

'It was real Heidi; it was so bloody real.' I sob.

'Dreams can be like that.' She smiles. 'I once had a dream where I was covered in spiders, it was hideous. I had to jump in the shower because I thought the buggers were still on me.'

'You haven't heard anything on the news?'

'I haven't. And if I had, my first priority wouldn't have been peeing. It was just a nightmare, and it's hardly surprising considering what you've been through.'

'So, they're not alive?'

'Not to the best of my knowledge.'

Relief floods through me as I realise how stupid I've

been. Of course, it was a dream. It's not the first one I've had, so I should have known. It's just my mind playing tricks on me.

'Maybe...' Heidi begins, '...and I don't mean this in any other way than to be helpful to you. But maybe, you should see that therapist lady again. It helped before didn't it?'

'Well I only managed the one session the last time, before it all kicked off, but I remember at the time thinking that she would be able to help me.'

'There you go then. You don't have to tell her the full ins and outs of what's going on, in fact, the fewer people that know, the better. But you could get some general advice.'

She's right. I do need help, of a professional nature. I just now need to work out how the hell I get that help without confessing to murder.

Eight

Stella White looks at me like something that the cat has dragged in. Well, maybe not as disdainfully, but I can tell that she's somewhat put out by my appearance.

The dark bags under my eyes, my choppy hair which desperately needs the help of a professional and my blotchy red skin. Yes, I'm a mess. And in a place like this, where everyone, and I do mean everyone, is exceptionally well groomed, I stick out like the proverbial sore thumb.

It was good of her to fit me in at such short notice though, and as I sink into the chair by the window, I begin my costly hour-long session by asking her how I deal with nightmares.

'What kind of nightmares are we talking about here?' She asks while scribbling in her notepad. 'The kind where you find yourself suddenly naked in the street? Or maybe during an important meeting? Or even the kind where you feel like you are falling, flying, or being attacked? All of these types of dreams can be deciphered and…'

'The kind where the dead come back to life.' I interrupt.

'Okay.' She mumbles, again jotting something down in

her notebook. 'This could be a sign of many things. Survivor's guilt, unresolved issues with the person that's passed, or your own issues with death and loss. They can also often be interpreted as messages from the other side. Do you feel comfortable telling me the nature of the dream?'

'I... erm. Well, the thing is, I thought the nightmare was real, you know. That somebody bad, who I know is very much dead, was suddenly very much alive.'

'And was this person *bad* to you? I know in our last session you touched upon some sensitive and painful issues with your ex-husband?'

'This person was bad to me yes.' I answer, careful not to be drawn into anything that would involve discussing Eric.

'But this person is dead. So why are they haunting me?'

'Haunting is an interesting word choice.'

'What else could it be, if not haunting? They are dead and now they won't leave me alone.'

'Do you see this person when you're awake?'

'I'm not crazy!' I fume, 'I know that I'm dreaming.'

'I'm not suggesting for even a moment that you are crazy; I'm just trying to understand.' She sympathises, 'Do you feel like you have unresolved issues with this person? Things maybe that you wish you had said, or done?'

'So many things.' I sigh. 'But it's too late for that now. They're dead. I just want the nightmares to stop. Can you help me with that? Can you show me some trick to stop them?'

'There isn't a cure-all trick.' She smiles, sadly. 'But it's evident that there are a lot of unresolved issues here. Issues that you need to work through and deal with. You say that you wish you had said or done things differently when this person was alive, so why don't we start there.'

'How can I do that if they aren't here?'

'Do you feel comfortable telling me who they were to you?'

'No.' I shake my head furiously, 'No. I can't do that.'

'That's fine. We can work our way up to that.' She smiles again, 'would you be up for a little homework?'

'Homework?' I squeak. 'Will it stop the nightmares?'

'It could help somewhat with coming to terms with what has happened, which in turn should ease some of the anxiety and pressure you are currently experiencing.'

'Okay. What do I need to do?'

'I want you to write letters to this person, paying particular attention to how they made you feel. In these letters I want you to tell them exactly what you would have said if you could go back and do things differently.'

'And then what?'

'And then you burn them.'

'You want me to write letters and then set them on fire?'

'I know that it sounds a little *out there*. But I think you'll find that writing things down will put a lot of things in perspective for you and let a lot of those old emotions out. I think it will help; I do.'

'I guess it makes sense.' I shrug, willing to give anything a go at this point. 'Do I need to tell you what's in the letters?'

'No. These letters are just for you. Nobody else needs to see them or read them.'

'How many do I have to do?'

'As many as you feel you want to.'

'And then I just burn them?'

'And then you just burn them.'

~~Dear~~ Eric,

I knew you were bad news the moment that I set eyes on you. Oh sure, you were good-looking and charming, but beneath that shiny veneer was something dark, something evil. I just didn't realise how evil until it was too late.

I should have ignored your messages; I should have blocked your number. I should have erased you from my mind, because you broke me. You hurt me in ways that words cannot accurately describe.

What right did you have to do that to me?

What gave you the right to ruin my life?

You piece of shit!

My friends warned me about you and you turned me against them. Even they could see your darkness. They knew I was making a huge mistake.

I should have left you the moment that you stopped me from seeing my friends. When you belittled me and made me feel less than nothing. I should have left you the moment that you first raised a hand to me.

So many 'I should have' moments, and I regret them all.

I was weak, Eric, because you made me weak.

I no longer recognised the woman staring back at me in the mirror, and I certainly didn't recognise the woman who lost her voice. The woman that nodded and agreed with everything you said – just because it was safer that way.

You did that!

You!

You waltzed into my life and turned it upside down, all because I wasn't good enough for you.

Why then did you choose me, Eric?

If I was so stupid, so pathetic, so not right?

Why didn't you just stay away from me?

Why did you think you had any right to mould me into some twisted, feeble, pitiful version of myself, just to suit you?

Why?

Arranging your tins by content and hanging your clothes in colour order was a joke.

You were a joke!

Our wedding vows?

Pathetic!

I didn't mean one solitary word. How could I when I hated you. I hated your handsome face; I hated your fake charm and I hated how you thought women were beneath you. Just toys to be played with until you were bored.

I took the pill, Eric. I took the pill so you couldn't get me pregnant. So you weren't that smart after all, were you?

You thought there was something wrong with me. Did you ever stop to consider that maybe there was something wrong with you?

No, of course not. Not the almighty Eric Sawyer!

You have no idea how many times I prayed that you would die on your way to a business meeting. That you'd be involved in some horrible accident. I never wanted you to have an accident and end up wheelchair-bound like me. I just wanted you to die. I wanted you gone. Forever.

I guess I got my wish in the end.

I have healed from the slaps and the punches and I have healed from the many many times that you raped me, taking what you claimed was your right. But it will take me a long time to heal from what you did to me mentally.

Maybe that pleases you, that you still have a hold on me, that you can still hurt me even from the grave.

But I am stronger than you ever gave me credit for.

I am a survivor.

I have proven this to myself time and time again, and I will continue to prove it to myself while you rot in some unknown well on some unknown land.

Nobody cares that you are gone, Eric!

I've watched the news, and read the papers, and not one single person cares enough to report you missing. The big almighty Eric Sawyer doesn't even warrant one line in a newspaper.

It would be so terribly tragic if you hadn't been such a bastard!

I have my life back now Eric. It may not be the life that I had before. But it's a life free from you. Free from your abuse.

And what do you have?

An unmarked grave and nobody to mourn you.

Who's the pathetic one now, Eric?

Jade <u>Locke.</u>

Dear Jake,

I am so sorry.

Jade.

Nine

*T*he *Dirty Rabbit* is heaving as we push our way through the crowd to get to the bar. It's my first night out with the girls since coming home, and to say that I'm excited would be a major understatement.

Tonight, there will be no men, aside from Gordon of course. We have no interest in that tonight. We plan only to drink, dance and sing – we plan only to be single and happy!

Tonight *The Dirty Rabbit* is hosting a karaoke competition and normally I would need to be at least six drinks in before I even contemplated making a fool of myself – but not this evening. This evening I don't care who hears me sing (screech) my way through some cheesy pop track – this evening I can do whatever the hell I like.

'Oh, God.' Heid groans as she thrusts a drink into my hand. 'Are we doing it? Really? Don't you want a few more of these bad boys first?'

'What even is this?' I ask as I take a sniff.

'No idea.' She shrugs, 'I just asked them to make us something *different*.'

Taking a large mouthful, I laugh, 'Yep, Heids, it's definitely different! Let's order four more!'

'Yes!' She bellows. 'This is the Jade that I know and love – drink any man or woman under the table! Barman? We'll have six more of… whatever the hell this rat poison is.'

'Come on.' I laugh as I pull her towards the karaoke machine, 'let's do this.'

'I am nowhere near drunk enough for this shit.' She sighs, 'but okay, whatever.'

'Got another two mics there?' Nicky giggles as she and Jess make their way over. 'We can do a…. what's the word for four people?'

'A quartet.' Gordon replies as he grabs a table at the front. 'And God help us all.'

'We can be *Little Mix*!' laughs Jess as she begins flicking through the book to find the perfect song, which we are inevitably going to ruin. 'Okay, I got it!'

As the music starts and I instantly recognise the song, I can't help but chuckle. 'Bold choice, Jess. Very bold.'

'Oh yeah!'

The song of course is '*Shout Out to My Ex*' and as we all croon along to the lyrics, I can't remember a time that I've ever felt this free, this liberated.

"Shout out to my ex, you're really quite the man,
You made my heart break and that made me who I am.
Here's to my ex, hey, look at me now,
Well, I'm, I'm all the way up,
I swear you'll never, you'll never bring me down.

Oh, I deleted all your pics,
Then blocked your number from my phone,
Yeah, yeah, you took all you could get,
But you ain't gettin' this love no more.
'Cause now I'm living so legit,
Even though you broke my heart in two, baby,
But I snapped right back, I'm so brand new, baby,
Boy, read my lips, I'm over you."

To the somewhat sarcastic yet amused applause of Gordon and a few of the regulars, we each take a bow, pleased with our drunken, yet rather fabulous (in our humble opinion) performance and make our way once more towards the bar. Heidi is determined to make a proper night of it, and as she lines up the shots I excuse myself and nip quickly to the ladies.

The corridor is dark as I navigate my way down two flights of stairs and into the bowels of the pub. I wonder again, as I do every time I come here – why the toilets are so bloody far away, why Barry, the landlord never ever replaces the bulb, and why in God's name anyone would think it's a good idea to let drunk people anywhere near steps - in the dark!

I know that I am well on my way to having the hangover from hell tomorrow, and as I bounce off the walls trying to locate the handle to the ladies' toilets, I freeze, as hot breath ripples across the back of my neck.

Swinging around I try to make out the person breathing on me, the person that thinks it's okay to creep up on unsuspecting women, but I can't. Not because it's almost pitch black down here, and not because I am so tipsy that I'm struggling to see straight, but because there's nobody there. Just me and the never-ending darkness.

'Hello?' I squeak. 'Who's there?'

I can hear someone breathing and yet I cannot see them.

'Heidi, is that you? It isn't funny, okay!'

Stretching my arms out in front of me, I tremble at the thought of what my fingertips may find, or worse, what fingertips may find me.

'Heids? C'mon.' I plead, as I wave my arms at absolute nothingness. 'This really isn't funny.'

It's odd, how your senses alter in certain situations. I can barely see, and yet my hearing is super tuned. I can hear breathing; I know I can.

'Heidi? I am not nearly drunk enough for this!'

Maybe I should go back, check if it is one of the girls messing with me, because if it isn't...

'Who's there?' I demand, as my bladder screams at me, desperate as I am to pee and as the weird breathing continues. I could just go back, it'll only take a moment, but I know I'll never make it there and back again without having an *accident.*

'You know what?' I yell into the shadows, 'I am way too pissed for this shit. You, whoever you are...' I laugh nervously, '...can hang around dingy corridors all you like, but I need to pee. Goodbye!'

Swinging on my heel, I bounce along the wall until I locate the door for the ladies' loos and tumble inside. There is at least a light in here, and despite being momentarily blinded by its brightness, I feel relieved at the sight of it.

Quickly using the facilities, I wash my hands and stare at myself in the mirror, psyching myself up for the return journey back to the bar.

'You can do this, Jade.' I whimper to my reflection, 'It's just a corridor, it's just dark, it's just a few seconds, you can do this!'

Taking a deep breath I throw open the door and walk as fast as my wobbly-heeled feet will allow, concentrating on nothing but the sound of the music booming from the bar, and the very strong words I plan to have with Barry about the health and safety issues in this bloody corridor!

I can see the bar now. Jess and Nicky are dancing together to some cheesy 80's track, while Heidi and Gordon have their heads together talking rather animatedly about something or other, and as I raise my arms above my head to wave at them and announce my return in some flamboyant fashion, I am suddenly grabbed from behind and pulled once more into the gloom.

Before I can scream, a rough calloused hand slams itself against my face as I am pushed violently against the wall and my attacker plunges his hand beneath my dress.

I don't know what to do.

My body has frozen, and even though I know that I need to move, to scream, to fight back, my brain has powered down. It's like all of the other moments that I have suffered through, all of those moments where I was too frightened to move, to speak, to scream - and yet, I realise with sudden clarity, that even in the darkness of all of those other moments, I survived!

I bloody survived!

Raising my knee I aim it directly at his groin and as he doubles over in shock and pain, I stumble away from him, shaken but not beaten.

Pulling down my dress I begin to make my way back toward the bar, but am stopped once again as my attacker grabs my arm and roughly yanks me up against his body.

'That wasn't very nice Jade.' He snarls in my ear as I try to wriggle out of his steely embrace. 'Not very nice at all.'

'Ben?' I gasp, as my mind tries to catch up with all that is happening. 'What the…'

'I know you've done something to Eric.' He slurs, 'I know…'

'Jesus Christ!' I snap, 'will you let this go! I don't know where he is and I don't care! Let me go!'

'Which…' he continues as though I haven't spoken, '…makes you fair game.'

'What do you mean fair game? Are you out of your mind?'

'The way I see it, you don't belong to anyone, anymore – so I might as well pick up where Eric left off.'

'I never belonged to him!' I spit, 'I'll never belong to anyone! What is with you and him? You think you can do whatever you please, you…'

'*I can do* whatever I please.' He snarls. 'And with Eric gone, I plan to do a lot. To you.'

'It just breaks my heart how much you miss him.' I hiss as I try in vain to wriggle free of his grasp. 'Not gone two minutes and you're trying to muscle in on his wife. You must be hurting *so* bad!'

'Well, waste not, want not, eh, Jade?'

As he reaches beneath my dress once more, I open my mouth to scream, and he laughs in my face, his beer breath making me recoil as it wafts into my nostrils, 'they can't hear you Jade, not from so far away…'

'Good job I'm not so far away then, isn't it?' Gordon bellows from somewhere behind me, and Ben is suddenly thrown backwards.

'You lay your hands on my best friend again….' screeches Heidi as she waves her beautifully manicured finger in Ben's face, '…and you won't have any hands left, got it?!'

My legs feel like jelly as the reality of all that has happened begins to sink in. What would have happened if they hadn't turned up?

With one muscly arm holding onto a furious Ben, Gordon looks at me, concern etched all over his big handsome face, and I am frozen.

How many more times must he save me?

How many more times must he be my hero?

'Are you okay?' he smiles.

I can't speak, as I stare at Gordon and he stares at me.
'I...'

'Yeah?'

'Okay.' Heidi interrupts, '*we* are heading back to the bar because more drinks are definitely in order right now. And *you...*' she jabs at Ben again, '...you are about to be very sorry for what you just did!'

'She did something to Eric!' Ben screams as he tries to clamber out of Gordon's vice-like grip, 'She...'

Ben's words fade out as Gordon drags him into the darkness of the never-ending corridor, and as I turn to face Heidi, the only person in the world who knows the truth, I sob. 'He...'

'He knows shit! He's pissed, stupid and an arsehole! C'mon.' She smiles as she helps me walk unsteadily back to the bar, 'we have some drinking to do.'

Ten

Peeling open my crusty dry eyes, I wince at the pounding in my head. My mouth feels like a well-worn flip-flop, and the nausea – don't even get me started on the nausea.

Last night had been wonderful, despite that twit Ben trying to ruin it. I now know for certain that he will not let me be and that his threats had not been idle, despite Gordon 'having a word.' I just know that I haven't seen or heard the last of him.

However, the girls had not allowed me to dwell on all that had happened and soon the shots were flowing and shoes were kicked off as we danced the night away. Ben and his scary intimidation tactics were all but forgotten – for one night anyway.

After so many years of dreaming of a night like that, after the many hours of looking at myself in the mirror with my red lipstick on, nothing could have prepared me for just how marvellous it had been.

To dance and sing and be merry.

It had exceeded all of my expectations.

There was something though. Something that I'm not

sure now was just a figment of my drunken imagination. But I feel like something passed between me and Gordon last night. Something unexpected.

There was a moment. Ever so fleeting, where our eyes met and time just sort of stopped. I can't explain it. He looked at me and I looked at him and it was like when you see someone for the very first time, when you *really* see someone.

When you know that being *friends* just isn't going to work anymore, where you seem able to see into one another's soul and sparks fly...

Gagging, I run for the bathroom and shove my head into the toilet bowl, as last night's frivolity makes a rather hasty reappearance.

God, how much did I drink last night?

What is this Mills & Boon shit that I'm spouting?

I must still be drunk.

It's Gordon for crying out loud!

I've looked into his eyes a million times over the years. Nothing. No soul diving. No Sparks. No nothing! Because it's Gordon! He's Heidi's brother!

Jesus, he's practically *my* brother!

I need to lay off the Sambuca.

Eleven

There is nothing on the news.

Work has been great since I started back at the souvenir shop, it's been good to get back out there and mingle with the locals and the tourists. A lot of the regulars have asked where I've been, and I told them, away. I've just been away. I feel like life is finally settling down for me. I enjoy quiet nights in, reading or watching movies on Netflix, and of course the occasional rowdy night out with the girls.
Life is simple now and some people might find that boring, a little dull, but it suits me to the ground.

Dull is good.

No drama is good.

I know of course that it won't last. I know that what I have done, and what I have seen, will catch up with me eventually. But now, in this moment, I have a little of the peace that I so desperately craved during my marriage and I plan to enjoy it for as long as I have it.

It's nice, you know, just to sit and not worry that I've done something wrong, to not stress that I'm about to be blamed for something stupid, something pointless. To not watch the clock and wonder when he will be home and what mood he will be in.

It's nice just to sit.

Heidi checks on me every day, even though I've told her countless times that I'm doing well – she just won't believe me until she hears me say it.

I am thankful for Heidi. She has stood by me even though there were times that she could quite easily and understandably have given up on our friendship. I am glad that she didn't. I would be lost without her.

She knows that I haven't told her everything, and yet, despite her curiosity, and her need to understand, she never asks me. She knows that I will tell her, when the time is right, when I feel strong enough to go back there.

Until then, she remains a loyal friend. A sister.

I've managed to avoid Ben, which is partly because I keep a hawk eye out for him, and also because I stay home most nights now, learning again how to enjoy my own company and my own space. If he's still adamant about stalking me then he's in for a long wait.

I ordered my bookcase and it looks lovely in my lounge. I am also very much enjoying filling the shelves with fiction of every kind imaginable.

I still haven't had my lemon top ice cream or a paddle in the sea, but they are next on my list of things to do.

I have a new bed, I've stripped the wheelchair down and taken it to the local tip, I'm going to redecorate the whole house, something bright and colourful I think, and despite Eric's stuff gathering dust under the spare bedroom bed, I feel fine.

Yes.

I feel fine.

I feel fine!

There is nothing on the news.

Twelve

Christmas Eve has come around at an alarming rate, and as the girls and I shop for Christmas presents, drink mulled wine and sing carols with the buskers that are out and about in Whitby town centre, I can't help but remember the Christmas when everything changed from bad to worse.

The day I was hit by a car and hospitalised.

The day that gave Eric even more control over me.

Yet another day that I somehow survived.

It seems like a lifetime ago that I was wheelchair-bound and even more under the control and mercy of my crazed husband, and for the life of me, I cannot understand how I ever made it out of there – to be standing here now – singing! It doesn't compute – the woman then, to the woman now.

I can't dwell on the past however, because this Christmas is all about friends and family, and I plan to make the most of it.

I'm still feeling a little bit peculiar about Gordon and will admit that I'm somewhat nervous about seeing him, but as my parents are hosting Christmas dinner this year, and everyone is invited, I can't very well avoid him.

I can't even discuss this madness with my best friend, she would think it was totally gross and then I'd never hear the end of it.

I know that I can't avoid him, but I can pretend that everything is normal. Acting is something that seems to come naturally to me these days, so as long as I make out that nothing has changed, then nobody will suspect a thing. Easy? Right?

I have watched the news religiously since my return and not one channel has announced the disappearance of two men and they certainly haven't announced two dead bodies being found. I had considered returning to the summer house, just to check, just to make sure that they are both still very much in there. But that would be stupid! I can't go anywhere near that house or that well. It's done. I am done. It happened and there is nothing that I can do about it.

It sounds cold, I know. Callous even. But what choice do I really have? Sink into despair, take up daytime drinking, let myself go, or make the most of what I have now?

So my plan is simple.

My plan now is to live my best life.

I am free and I plan to stay that way.

Single. Free. Myself.

'Earth to Jade, Earth to Space Cadet?' Chuckles Heidi as she gives me a nudge, 'What are you getting Gordon for Christmas?'

Ugh!

Thirteen

Christmas day and mum has really gone to town! As I push open the front door, my senses are instantly overloaded with the scent of turkey, Christmas pud and... what is that? A mulled wine diffuser?

'Merry Christmas', I holler, cheerily as I avoid the spray from the diffuser, coughing a little as it sprays out a little burst of Christmas joy that hits the back of my throat. 'You all in the kitchen?'

'Come on through, love.' Dad hollers back, 'we're all in here... mum is making cocktails.'

Oh god! Not the cocktails!

Poking my head into the kitchen I have to laugh at the utter chaos before me. Mum is doing her best impression of *Tom Cruise* in *Cocktail*, while Heidi is merrily sampling all of the mistakes. Dad is adding icing to his homemade mince pies, while Nicky and Jess are playing some strange game that involves throwing squishy balls at Velcro strips that they each have on their heads. And then there's Gordon. Gordon is busy setting the table and humming away to the music playing on the Alexa.

Dumping my bag of gifts onto the floor, I hug everyone in turn, hesitating only slightly when I reach Gordon.

'Hey, trouble.' He grins, as he pulls me into his arms 'that big bag all for me?'

'Ha. You wish. Yours is the little bag, inside the big bag.'

'Yeah? Well, all good things come in small packages.'

'Hmm, just like me.'

'Exactly like you.' He grins.

'Can I do anything?' I ask mum, as I avoid Gordon's gaze and instead stupidly join Heidi in the cocktail tasting. They have definitely not improved.

'No, no. You sit yourself down. Dinners nearly ready and then we'll do gifts.'

I've always loved Christmas. Everyone just seems happier, like we've all been sucked into a bubble of jovial, carefree bliss.

I love the fairy lights, tinsel, foil decorations hung from the ceiling, chocolate coins hidden in the Christmas tree, the food, the wine, the chance to over indulge – because everyone knows that calories don't count at Christmas. But most importantly I love this… the banter and the laughing, cheesy jokes, everyone just being together – chaotic but perfect.

Dinner over – it was yet another spectacular masterpiece by mum - we all make our way into the lounge, zips and belts undone to make room for even more treats, and the gift exchange begins.

The rather large, heavy box that Heidi had attempted to deliver to Bardsey – my gift from Gordon – is a huge box of books, no wonder it weighs a tonne.

'Gordon, this is fabulous.' I gush, as I scan through them all, 'thank you, I love it.'

'Picked them all out himself.' Heidi laughs. 'With about a thousand text messages to me! And as you know, I don't read, so I wasn't that helpful!'

'You picked these?' I ask now, as I pick out the last book in the box. My all-time favourite book (after Molly's Millions), and the one book I re-read every year - *P.S. I Love You*. But he could never have known that. Could he?

'I did.' He shrugs. And despite his nonchalance, he has a slight blush creeping up from beneath his shirt collar.

Did he know it's my favourite book?

Or does it mean something else entirely?

Placing the book at the very top of the pile now, I try to shake off the thoughts running through my mind.

It doesn't mean anything – it's a popular book – it's not a declaration of actual love, Jade! And even if it was, do I even want that? With Gordon?

'Here.' I smile, as I pass Gordon his gift from me. 'It's not as amazing as your gift, but I hope you like it.'

My gift to Gordon is a vinyl record of his favourite band – AC/DC. And as it's a first pressing it was a tad on the pricey side. But what else can you buy the man who has everything?

'Jade!' He exclaims loudly as his gift is unwrapped. 'This is too much; it must have cost a mint!'

Shrugging myself this time, I smile back, aware of my own blushes now, and laugh, 'like a fiver on Ebay.'

He knows of course that it didn't cost five pounds – but he laughs along anyway, evidently delighted with his gift.

Something has shifted between us, something that I most certainly hadn't contemplated. And I don't know how I feel about it. How does that happen? One minute you're just sailing along happily, and then…

And then what?

It was a box of books – get over it!

It means nothing!

The rest of the day passes in a blur of laughter, too much food, the standard cheesy Christmas movie, Christmas crackers and yes, even more food! Heidi is snoring loudly on the sofa as mum and dad bicker good-naturedly - This has been the best Christmas that I have had in a long long time, and I can't help but feel happy.

Slightly confused, but happy.

Fourteen

Pushing open the front door, laden with gifts and leftover food, I kick the door shut behind me and walk blindly into the kitchen. How on earth mum thinks I'm going to eat all of this is beyond me. There's enough here to feed an army! I'll take some of it to the homeless shelter tomorrow, that way I can be helpful with this mountain of food and also not feel guilty that I haven't eaten it.

Mum never needs to know.

It's been a long day and I can feel the familiar twinge of a migraine coming on, and as I stifle a yawn I know that I won't be long out of bed.

Dropping my goodies onto the kitchen table, I turn to flick on the light, but immediately know that something is wrong here – something is ever so slightly, off!

'Merry Christmas, Jade.' The man's voice behind me freezes me in my tracks, turning my blood to ice, and my legs to jelly. 'Looks like you've had a nice day.'

This isn't real. This isn't real.

Facing the man now, I gasp as I take in the sight before me. Maggots, so many maggots, wriggling across my floor, and the blood – oh god, the blood!

Screaming, I cover my face with my hands – I won't look. I won't.

'What's wrong Jade? Am I not how you remembered me? I wonder why that is?'

This isn't real. This is real!

'LOOK AT ME!' he screams now, as I drop my hands from my face and stare at the man that I killed. 'You look exactly as I remember you. You look like a cold heartless bitch, Jade!

'Jake, I…'

'Don't tell me you're sorry. What a joke! I tried to help you, didn't I? And what did I get in return? Why did you kill me, Jade? Why?'

Sobbing, I sink to my knees, this isn't real. It isn't.

'WHY?' he yells again, 'WHY?'

'BECAUSE YOU WERE JUST LIKE HIM!' I scream back, 'because you were just like him!'

'Do you really believe that? Or is that what you tell yourself to make it all okay? I helped you that night, and you turned on me. I was innocent!'

'You were not! You were just like him – I know you were! It was only a matter of time before you showed your true colours! You were just like him!'

'Yeah, you keep telling yourself that.' He smirks, 'Deep down though, Jade, you know it's all bullshit. You know you can't live with this lie. So tell me this Jade, just what will it take for you to come clean? To admit that you butchered an innocent man? What will it take, Jade?!'

'You weren't innocent.' I sob, 'you weren't.'

'I was, and you know it!'

Shoving myself from the bed, I try desperately to pull air into my lungs as a small whimper escapes my throat. Another nightmare? Is that what it was? I don't even recall getting into bed.

I remember dumping mum's leftovers onto the table. I remember the start of a headache, but I absolutely cannot recall getting into bed!

Was I so exhausted that I forgot? I just climbed into bed without even realising that I'd done it? I know that I'm suffering from stress and fatigue, who wouldn't be in this situation? But surely not memory loss too!

The alternative of course is that I never went to bed at all, and last night was some crazed hallucination, but, I'm not prepared to accept that I am seeing things that aren't there. I'm not crazy. I'm not!

It's clearly just my guilty conscience playing tricks on

me, making me believe that I was wrong and they were right. But I *was* right. At least where Eric was concerned. Jake, however, I'm now not so sure about.

Could I have gotten it so monstrously wrong?
What if the Jake in my nightmare is right, and he was in fact innocent? That would mean that I didn't kill him in a desperate bid to free myself once more, because I was afraid, because I was petrified that he too would hold me against my will, a prisoner for a second time – it would mean that I killed him in cold blood for no other reason than I wanted to. Because I could.

<u>13th March 2026</u>

~~*Peyton Gray*~~

F.A.O Jade ~~Locke~~ Sawyer

This letter may come as a shock to you, I am in no doubt at all that you think you are home-free. That the devastation you've caused and the lives you have ruined are no longer at the forefront of your mind, so I'm here to remind you.
I know what you did.
You think you can run and hide from that.
You can't.
Your secrets are about to see the light.
You however will only see the darkness.
You lied.
You deceived.
You will pay.

I'll be seeing you!

Fifteen

The letter can only be from someone in Bardsey.

From the moment that I discovered it lying on my doormat, I've known that I am now very much living on borrowed time and that someone I believed to be my friend in Bardsey is now threatening me.

The letter was not stamped and postmarked; it was simply addressed to me (well, various versions of me) which means that whoever wrote this note has really done their homework. They know where I live, my maiden name, that I was married and they've also stood outside my home with the most sinister of intentions.

Did they post it while I was sleeping?

Have they been watching me?

Am I even safe?

I assumed at first that maybe it was Ben who posted the letter. But he knows me only as 'Jade', and as the letter contains the name 'Peyton', which he could never have known about – it makes perfect sense that it must be someone from Bardsey.

I have racked my brain over and over, but I am no

closer to understanding who could have sent such a menacing note. The ladies that I socialised with in Bardsey were not like this, they weren't the type to post threats designed to intimidate and frighten me. They were all so pleasant, so, well, *villagey*.

We were alone that night, the three of us. So how could anybody possibly know what transpired? I am the only person who walked out of there – the only person on this planet that could ever know what truly happened – so how is this even possible?

The only person that I can imagine having such a vivid imagination, or a motive of sorts, is Jemima.

The last time that I saw her was in Munchies café and the ladies were ribbing her about the book that she's allegedly writing. Could she have followed me? Has she taken her *gossip book* to a whole new level and is now in fact writing the truth? Jemima is nosey, that is true, but would she sink to these depths just to write a book?

I just can't see it.

Heidi was shocked when I showed her the note, then she panicked a little and then she got mad. Making it clear that no *little old dear* was going the threaten me and get away with it. She even jangled her car keys in my face and suggested, or rather commanded, that we head to Bardsey right away and find the culprit.

I had chuckled, nervously, but she was deadly serious!

So, that's what we are going to do.

We are heading back to Bardsey!

Sixteen

'Well, knock me down with a fluffy white feather – is that you Peyton?' Dorothy asks as she peers out at me over her new and rather funky purple spectacles. 'Where in the name of the sweet baby Jesus have you been? Is Jake with you?'

I knew that I would be asked questions, of course I did, and I was prepared, but now that I'm here facing them my mind has gone blank. I don't want to lie to Dorothy, I don't, but what choice do I have? It's also a shock to the system to hear the name Peyton once more, but without confessing to everything, I will always be Peyton here in Bardsey.

Heidi already knows about my name change, and I've filled her in on who is who, so she doesn't even bat an eyelid when I'm addressed as Peyton – she just goes with it.

'No... I erm... Jake and I went our separate ways. This is Heidi.' I smile, 'my best friend.'

'I did wonder.' She smiles. 'Of course, you know what it's like, everybody has had something to say, not me of course, you know I don't get involved in all of that chit-chat. But, there was a rumour, speculation really, that you and Jake had eloped. It's lovely to meet you, Heidi.' She grins, 'You're a bonnie one, aren't you.'

'Good genes.' She shrugs, not at all impressed with Dorothy. I don't think Heidi will be impressed with anyone here until we work out who is threatening me.

'Eloped?' I gasp, 'why on earth would anybody think that?'

'You were cosy.' She winks. 'Even I thought for just a moment that it might be true.'

Sighing, I lean against the doorframe and shake my head, 'Jake and I didn't elope. I haven't seen him since I left Bardsey.' I lie, 'Our relationship, or whatever it was, just wasn't meant to be.'

It would also explain why nobody has reported him missing, I muse. They all just assumed we had run away together.

'That is a shame.' She sighs, 'though between you and me, our sweet little Clara will be secretly pleased I'm sure.'

'Oh? Why's that?'

'She's always had a soft spot for Jake, not that she'd ever have been brave enough to tell him mind you.'

'I didn't know that. I hope that she didn't think I was

stepping on her toes, I truly had no idea.'

'Don't be silly. She wouldn't have been right for him anyway, she's much too timid. And no, she never said anything about the two of you being together, before you ask. Certainly not to me anyway.'

'Okay. Well, I can only apologise if I've caused her any upset. I'll speak to her today if I get the chance.'

'I wouldn't bother dearie, she hasn't mentioned him or his disappearing act, so she's no doubt moved on from her small infatuation.'

'*Infatuation*? That's a little more than just a *crush*.' Heidi questions, with a frown.

'Wrong word choice dearie.' She laughs, 'it really was just a passing fancy.'

'If you say so.' She scowls.

'I hope so.' I smile, awkwardly as I give Heidi a quick jab with my elbow. I know she's pissed off, but we need Dorothy on side, just until we figure out what on earth is going on.

Glaring at me once more over the rim of her glasses Dorothy changes the subject entirely and asks if I've changed my hair, and as I subconsciously reach up to touch it she frowns, 'I can't say that I like it dearie, but, maybe it will grow on me. No pun intended of course.'

She chuckles.

'*I* like it.' Sulks Heidi, as she rubs her side, and I hold back a chuckle, because I know that Heidi most certainly doesn't like it, in fact, I know it makes her madder than hell.

'How is everyone?' I ask, purposely sidestepping her query about my new and not-at-all-improved hairdo, 'I thought I might catch up with a few people while I'm over this way.'

'Well, I was just on my way over to the café actually to meet the ladies, if *you* want to come along?'

Dorothy clearly does not like Heidi and she isn't making any effort to disguise that fact.

'What a great idea.' Heidi grins, '*We* would love to.'

As Heidi marches ahead of us towards the café, I glance around nervously at the village that was once my saviour, my hiding place, my second chance. Nothing has changed. It's still as sweet and peaceful as it was when I left. Only now, returning, I know that this calm, tranquil little hamlet harbours a dark secret and that any one of the lovely ladies that I am going to see again, in just a few moments, could be planning to harm me, and I am afraid.

I am very afraid.

Seventeen

Pushing open the door to the café, I see instantly that Heidi has already ingratiated herself within the group, and as I knew she would be, is happily making small talk, while she susses out the people in front of her.

Dorothy, however, looks less than impressed, and as I order our drinks, I glance over at the table in the corner, by the window and see that they are all here.

Sally, Jemima, Clara.

One of these women is my letter writer, and for the life of me, looking at them now, I can't imagine who it could be. Sally is the first to see me and shout a cheery hello across the café, closely followed by Jemima, and as I set our drinks down on the table and take a seat I can't help but notice how Clara seems to be avoiding eye contact with me.

Clara as we all know is painfully shy, but she knows me, we've spoken before, laughed even, around this very table. I can only surmise then that she is hurt, that she feels betrayed by me and my relationship with Jake.

Or, she's struggling to face the person that she's

threatened now that she's here in person.

Jemima, Sally, and Dorothy are chatting away as normal, throwing the odd question my way, and it doesn't take Heidi long to notice that the one person not speaking to me is Clara.

'Hi', she grins as she thrusts her face into Clara's. 'You're Clara, right? You're being awfully quiet, not going to say hello to your friend?'

'I, erm…'

Cringing, I watch helplessly as Clara begins to blush, as her face slowly turns pink.

'She's sitting right there.' Heidi continues, not at all oblivious to Clara's discomfort. 'C'mon, it's just one little word, you can do it.'

'Erm…'

'No? Okay.' She shrugs, as she raises an eyebrow at me, 'So what's everybody been up to? Any goss? Read any good books lately?'

'Jemima's writing a book.' Clara squeaks, 'A juicy one. It'll probably be a best seller and end up on the front pages of the newspapers.'

'Let's not start that again.' Dorothy frowns. 'We put this to bed a while ago.'

'So, where have you been Peyton?' Sally asks, in a

clear attempt to steer the conversation away from the book that everyone *just hates* discussing. 'One minute you were here and then poof. Gone. Is Jake with you?'

'Oh, just around, and no, we're no longer together.' I smile. 'We went our separate ways a while ago.'

'Aaw that's a shame. We all thought you were for keeps.'

'Yeah, shame.' Mumbles Clara, who is still very much avoiding eye contact with me.

'Well, life doesn't always play along with what we want, does it?'

'Strange though, that he hasn't been home, don't you think?' She continues with one perfectly raised eyebrow. 'I'd have thought with your relationship ending, he'd have come right back home to lick his wounds.'

'I don't know what to tell you.' I shrug as casually as I can. 'Maybe he went home to his parents for a little while?'

I can't ask outright why nobody cares that Jake is missing, but, knowing these women as I do, I can go around the houses and try and find out as much information as I can that might give me an idea.

'Oh, I very much doubt that.' Dorothy frowns, as she peers at me over her glasses once again. I wonder if this is something she's been practising in the mirror. 'They don't have the best of relationships.'

'Oh yes.' Sally squeaks, 'that's right. They had a bust-up over that girl, didn't they? It's all coming back to me now.'

'What girl is this?' I ask as I glare at Sally. The biggest gossiper in Bardsey suddenly realising that she's *just* remembered something. I bet she's known all along.

'Oh, it was a while ago now, if I'm getting my facts straight. Jake met some girl online and they had a brief fling.'

'So why would he fall out with his parents over that?'

'Well...' she starts again with obvious glee in her eyes, '...the relationship didn't end at all well. She accused him of cheating, he accused her of being too needy, ooh the arguments that they had out there in that very street were really something to behold, anyway...' she takes a breath, '...she left and then turned up a year later with a baby girl claiming that it was his. He denied it of course, so she reached out to his parents. They naturally wanted him to accept responsibility for this child, their grandchild, but he flat-out refused. Said it wasn't his, no way. Their relationship has been rocky ever since.'

'Why didn't he just get a DNA test and prove it wasn't his?'

'Because as far as he was concerned the baby was not his and he didn't feel like he had to prove that to anyone.'

'So where is she now? This ex and the baby?'

'Nobody knows for sure. After the last argument, she upped and left. Hasn't been back since. I have a feeling though that his parents are helping to support the child and that's why their relationship is so fractured.'

'He should have done his duty!' snaps Dorothy. 'I like Jake, I do. But I was disappointed in him. I was.'

'So, he's not in regular contact with them? His mum and dad?' I ask, tentatively.

'Oh, sure, birthday cards, Christmas presents, that sort of thing, but they don't visit. They have a nice place in East Keswick and I think he stays there sometimes when they're away. It's sad really, but, he wouldn't step up.'

'Maybe he *was* firing blanks and it wasn't his kid.' Heidi remarks as she glances around the table, 'Maybe he was too embarrassed to say anything.'

'Wow, I didn't know anything about any of this. Why didn't you tell me?' I question now, ever so slightly frustrated with the lot of them.

'It wasn't our place, dearie.' Dorothy smiles, sadly. 'I felt certain that Jake would tell you in his own time.'

'So that isn't why you broke up then?' Sally asks. 'No big

drama, no dumping him in disgust?'

'No. It was all perfectly amicable.' I respond, as confidently as I can, 'I had no idea about any of this.'

'But you *have* broken up? Surely there's more to it than what you're saying.'

'There isn't. There honestly isn't any story here.'

Sally, in her rightful place of village gossip really has the bit between her teeth on this one, and as I glance quickly at Heidi for a way out of this questioning, I see her mentally gearing up for another confrontation.

'Talking of stories…' Heidi shuffles closer to Jemima and gives her a little nudge. '…and not of the sperm donor kind, what exactly is this book that you're writing, Jem? Fiction? Poetry? Self Help? *Biography*?'

'Oh, the book, it's nothing really, just a few ideas that I'm playing around with.' She shrugs.

'C'mon.' Heidi laughs, 'Don't sell yourself short. I'm sure it's tough writing a book, especially a *juicy* one.'

'It isn't a juicy one.' She snaps, 'it's nothing.'

'Here we go again.' Dorothy sighs, as she takes a long sip of her coffee. 'This bloody book.'

'It *is* juicy.' Sally laughs, 'really juicy.'

'I wouldn't want to bore you.' Jemima whispers as she avoids eye contact with Heidi.

'You won't bore me.' She smiles.

'I would honestly. Let's just leave it, okay.'

'You won't bore me. Let's just have a little taster and then we can give you some feedback.'

'I couldn't.'

'Seriously. *I insist.*'

'That's enough of this nonsense.' Dorothy snaps as she slams her coffee cup down onto the table. 'The speculation regarding this so-called book is over. If there is a book, fine. We will all read it when it's released. But other than that, no more, okay?'

'Wow, this book must be a real shocker, Jemima. Look how hot and bothered you've got everybody.'

'You're the one that started this.' Clara pipes up. 'We don't even care about the book, not really. Sorry Jemima.'

Turning to face her, Heidi fixes her glare firmly on Clara's once again pink face, 'Oh I think you do care about the book. I think you all care about this book *a lot*. After all, you just said it's going to be a bestseller. What is it going to reveal Jemima, what secrets are you preparing to unleash?'

'I'm not preparing to unleash anything.' She stammers. 'It's nothing. Just a few ideas.'

'Seems like a few of you are riled up over *nothing* though

doesn't it?' Heidi continues. 'Who's your main character? Someone at this table?'

'I...'

'Enough!' Dorothy shouts, 'Peyton, it's been lovely to see you, it really has, but I think you and your friend should probably think about heading off now.'

'Ruffled a few feathers have I?' Heidi quips as she slurps down the last of her coffee. 'You never told me village life was so... interesting.'

'It isn't. Normally.' I sigh, realising that we are no closer to discovering who the mystery letter writer is.

'No. It isn't.' Dorothy fumes, 'only when outsiders make trouble unnecessarily.'

'Make trouble? By asking about a book? I sense that there are a lot of secrets in this sweet little village, and you four are right at the centre of them all.'

'C'mon Heids, let's get going. I think we've outstayed our welcome somewhat.'

'*You* will always be welcome, Peyton, dearie.'

'Ouch, that hurts me Dot, hits me right in the heart.' Heidi laughs as she moves towards the door. 'You know...' she grins, '...I love a good mystery, and a mystery is exactly what I've found here in tranquil little Bardsey. I'm going to enjoy very much unearthing it.'

Eighteen

'Do you think it's any of them?' I ask Heidi as we make our way back to the car. 'Did you get any vibes at all that one of them could be the one threatening me?'

'Nah.' She laughs. 'They're all just cuckoo batshit crazy village weirdos. There must be something in the air here. I mean let's tick them off; It's definitely not Clara, she's just pissy because you stole her man…'

'He wasn't *her* man…'

'Yeah, well she thinks he was. That's why she was giving you the evil eye the whole time.

Sally is just, well, blah!

Jemima is probably a closet fetishist, who swings naked from chandeliers, dresses up in leather on Sundays and whips her hubs with tea towels just for kicks. Her book is probably some true-life story of her filthy sexual antics. No wonder she doesn't want to share any spoilers!'

'Heidi, I don't think…'

'And Dorothy! Well, she's just a grumpy old busybody. It's none of them. They're too busy living in la la land to give a shit who you've bumped off.'

'Then who the hell is it?'

'I don't know. But it's none of those tight arses!'

'You really didn't like any of them? Not one?'

'Nope.' She grins. 'Too stuck up for my liking. You should be thankful you got out when you did.'

'It really wasn't like that when I lived here. They were all lovely to me.'

'I'm sure they were. *To your face.*'

'Well, that's nice.' I frown as I give her a playful little nudge. 'I'm just going to pop into the newsagent and grab some drinks for the drive back. You want anything else?'

'Yeah.' She grins. 'To return to the land of the living.'

Laughing, I push open the corner shop door, 'Five mins, okay.'

Grabbing two bottles of Coca-Cola and a couple of chocolate bars, I wander aimlessly up and down the aisles, waiting for the shop owner, who's currently out back unloading stock to acknowledge my presence.

There are no other customers in the shop, it's as silent as the rest of this village, and as I pick up items, read the labels and put them back down again, I smile at the simplicity of the action. Just having time to read a boring label is still a wonder to me. A wonder that I hope I never take for granted again. It's the little things for me that make me happy now and bring me peace. I don't need big grand gestures and fancy things – just five minutes to wander around a shop with nothing else on my mind other than what I plan to buy is pure bliss.

However, despite this moment of calm, I am very much looking forward to going back home. Being here makes me feel a little jittery. Like the whole place knows my secret. Like it's frowning at me – disapproving, disgusted. That I, Jade Locke should dare to taint its perfection. Who the hell do I think I am to ruin its illusion of tranquillity?! The sooner I'm back in Whitby, the better.

Making my way towards the back of the shop, to announce my presence, pay for my goods and get the hell out of this village once and for all, I freeze, as a face that I have looked upon too many times to count is suddenly and unexpectedly before me. As two eyes that I know almost as well as my own stare back at me, full of judgment.

I knew of course that this day would come.

I knew that he would return and bring about my downfall. He's back, here, right now and there's not a bloody thing that I can do about it!

Running from the shop with the newspaper crumpled between my shaking hands, I thrust the offending article at Heidi and collapse onto the bench.

'Jade, what the…?'

'Excuse me! Excuse me miss, you need to pay for those!'

Glancing up in horror, I see that I have been followed from the shop by the owner, and he looks less than impressed that I have made off with his stock. Yet another crime to add to my C.V of debauchery.

'Sorry. Sorry, I planned to, I've just had a shock that's all.'

'Hmm, I've heard that before.' He grumps as he holds his hands out for either the goods or the payment.

'Oh shut up!' Heidi snaps as she throws a two-pound coin in his direction. 'You can keep the change, for your troubles.'

'Well, there's no need for that! I should call the police. First, a theft, then verbal abuse, you tourists think you can just do whatever you like, well I…'

'No, no.' I plead. 'It was an honest mistake, I'm really sorry, please don't call the police, please.'

'Don't I know you?' He asks, as he eyeballs me. 'Yes, Yes I'm sure that I do.'

'She used to live here dipshit.' Heidi snaps. 'Christ, everyone in this village is nuts!'

Eyeballing me again, he removes his glasses and edges a little closer, 'Peyton, isn't it? I didn't recognise you straight away. You look…'

'Awful.' I shrug, 'I know. I am really sorry about these, have we paid you enough for them?'

'Well, no, not for the paper, drinks and chocolates, but it's okay, really.' He smiles now, as my slight indiscretion is seemingly brushed under the carpet, 'no harm done.'

'What?' Heidi snaps, 'no harm done….'

'Heids, it's okay, just leave it.'

'Fine.' She sulks, as she flops down onto the bench next to me, 'but *you* should maybe take a course in customer service!'

'Jesus, Heidi! Stop! I'm truly very sorry.' I smile at the shopkeeper, 'it's been a bit of a day and we're both a little highly strung.'

'Your friend certainly is.' He frowns, and I feel Heidi once again shaking with agitation. 'Like I said, no harm done. You have a good day now, Peyton.' He calls over his shoulder as he shuffles back into his shop, 'I hope that it improves.'

'Bloody hell, you really do know how to make a good first impression.' I snap.

'Yeah, well, nobody accuses my best friend of theft and

gets away with it!'

'Heidi, I did steal those things! Maybe not intentionally, but I did!'

'Whatever.' She shrugs. 'He was still an arsehole! What's got you so spooked anyway?'

'The paper Heids, look at the bloody paper!'

As her eyes skim the news report that is splashed all across the front page, she visibly recoils. 'Oh god!'

'I know!'

'How's this prick made the front page of the news?'

'I hardly think that's what we should be focusing on!'

'But still… the front page? And where'd they get this photo from? It's actually pretty decent for him.'

Looking closer now at the image of Eric, I realise it's the one from his business website. An image that appears friendly, trustworthy, and professional. All of the things that I know for certain Eric was not.

'This isn't good.' I sigh, 'It isn't good at all.'

~MISSING~
ACCOUNTANT VANISHES

Whitby News   Friday 3rd April 2026
By: Verity Cobain – News Reporter for the Whitby News

Police are today appealing for any information regarding the whereabouts of 34-year-old Accountant Eric Sawyer of Henrietta Street, Whitby.

Mr Sawyer is described as being of stocky build, 6ft 3' with dark brown hair and blue eyes.
Owner of Sawyer Inc. Mr Sawyer has ties to both Whitby and Leeds where he has a second home, used for business purposes whilst in the city.

Police do not suspect foul play, or that Mr Sawyer has come to any harm. We have been unable to speak with Mrs Sawyer concerning this report, but believe that she is currently in Whitby and is no doubt doing everything she can to help police locate her missing husband.

There have been no further updates in connection with this missing person enquiry since the time of publication. We will however keep our readers updated as the case progresses.

Verity Cobain – News Reporter for the Whitby News.

Nineteen

Reading the news report again, I focus on two things.

The first, Eric is only considered missing at this point. Second, the police do not suspect foul play.

'They haven't tried to contact me' I muse. 'The police. They haven't been in touch with me at all.'

'Probably because we've been here.' Heidi replies with a frown. 'I think we need to prepare ourselves for that conversation when we get back.'

'What do I say? What do I tell them?'

'Exactly what we planned. You split up, you went your separate ways, you came back to sort out a divorce and he was gone. You just assumed he'd left you. That's all you need to say. Nothing more, nothing less.'

'It's odd, don't you think?'

'What?'

'What Clara said. She said that the book Jemima is writing will probably be a best seller and end up on the front pages of the newspapers.'

'So?'

'You don't think it's weird that she said that and then all

of a sudden this story is on the front page?'

'I think *you* are odd. I think this whole *situation* is odd. But her comment and this newspaper are totally unrelated. You're seeing links that aren't there. It's just a coincidence. Just plain old boring coincidence.'

'Is it though?'

'Yep. Look, Clara is pissed at you, that much is obvious, but she's not telepathic Jade. How could she possibly have known that this story would be in the papers today? That you would be here, today?'

'Maybe she's already seen the news. Maybe she's tracking me! Maybe…'

'It's not Clara. She's a little mouse. She wouldn't have the balls to pull this off.'

'Well, they always say it's the quiet ones you have to watch out for.'

'Who says that Jade? Who?'

'I don't know. People.'

'People? *Okay*. All of this, it's just a coincidence. We need to concentrate on figuring out who the letter writer is and which of Eric's friends have reported him missing.'

'Well that's simple, isn't it. It has to have been Ben.'

'And why don't we think he's the letter writer?'

'How could he be?' I shrug, 'he didn't know about this

place, my name change, Eric finding me, the summer house, Jake.'

'Doesn't it stand to reason that if Eric could find you, Ben could as well?'

'If that was the case then surely he wouldn't have stood by while Jake smashed his bloody head in though?'

'Maybe he would.'

'Now who's the crazy one?!'

'No, no, hear me out. Ben has already made a beeline for you, more than once. His best friend is missing and he makes a play on his wife? Does that sound like a best friend to you?'

'Hmm, he did say that he and Eric used to discuss ways to hurt me. He even said that he suggested some of those things that he did to me.'

'So maybe, just maybe, he hoped to pick up where Eric left off?'

'But would he really watch as someone killed him?'

'Why not, you did.'

'Heidi! Jesus!'

'I'm just kidding.' She laughs, 'we have to laugh sometimes Jade, because this situation is getting way darker than either of us anticipated.'

'Maybe I should stay here. The police don't know about

this place, I could hide out…'

'You can't hide forever.'

'Maybe not forever, but for a little while.'

'I know that you want to run. I do. But we need to face this head-on, we need to give them as many reasons as we can to stop looking at you. We need to go home, Jade.'

Twenty

The police don't arrive at my front door until three days after our return to Whitby.

Three days of nail-biting tension.
Three days of barely any sleep.
Three days of considering turning myself in.

But when they finally do arrive I am strangely relieved.

Heidi asked me to let her know once they turned up so that she could be with me when I was questioned, and even now, as Detective Inspector Cole Shuter sits in my lounge, drinking my tea, eyeballing my life, I know that I will not call her.

Heidi is already embroiled in this mess much more than I would want her to be. For her to witness more of my lies is asking too much of her. It's asking too much of our friendship. She will of course be angry with me, but she will understand eventually that I am trying my best to protect her from the fallout of this.

My parents had of course seen the paper, as had Nicky and Jess and the phone calls and text messages had been relentless. So I stuck with the story that Heidi and I had hatched, which was simply that Eric had left me while I was in Bardsey. I didn't want to lie to them, of course I didn't, but too many people are already involved now or at the very least suspicious. And maybe, just maybe, If I tell the lie over and over again I might just begin to believe it myself.

I haven't seen or heard from Ben, but that doesn't mean anything. He's no doubt seen the paper and is hatching some cunning plan to catch me out, so the less ammunition I give him, the better.

'You're a difficult woman to get hold of Mrs Sawyer.' The detective begins with a smile. 'I thought for a moment that we might have a second missing person on our hands.'

'Please.' I smile back as I take a seat next to the detective. 'Call me Jade and I'm certainly not missing.'

'But your husband is.'

'Is he?'

'You don't believe so?'

'I don't know where my husband is. But, I also don't know whether or not that means he's missing.'

'Where do you think your husband is?'

'I don't know. Eric has many contacts and a lot of friends. I'm sure he's living his best life somewhere.'

'You don't seem concerned.' He frowns. 'Forgive me if

this comes across as a little blunt, but your husband has been reported missing, and not by you, his wife. You don't seem particularly bothered. Why would that be?'

'Eric and I were estranged. I left him three years ago. Our marriage was over.'

'Why was that Mrs… Jade?'

Sighing I lean further back into the couch, not because I'm comfortable, not because I'm relaxed, but because I need to play this right. I need this Detective Inspector to believe me, to read my body language – that of a woman not concerned, not fearful, not guilty.

'Our marriage ran its course. We had nothing left to give one another. I didn't love him and I wanted out. I haven't seen him for three years and I would have been happy never to see him again.'

'And yet you returned to the marital home – why is that?'

'Because it's my house. I own it.'

'And yet you left it. Walked away.'

'Barely.' I grimace. 'I knew that I would come home one day. All I hoped was that Eric would have seen sense, accepted our marriage was over and moved back to Leeds. I guess I was right.'

'What makes you think you're right?'

'I came back to ask Eric for a divorce. It was the only way

that I could think of to finally end things. To be able to move on. Our marriage was done, the paperwork was all that remained. I assumed he would have left, like I said, he has a place in Leeds. When I came back the house was empty. Why would I worry?'

'You didn't think to reach out to him? Make sure that he was in fact in Leeds?'

'No. My plan was simply to speak to a solicitor and ask them to send the paperwork to his other address.'

'And have you done that?'

'Not yet, no. I've had a few other things to deal with.'

'Such as?'

'Getting a job, reconnecting with my family and friends…'

'Normal stuff then.' He smiles.

'Exactly. Don't you think this is all a bit much? Assuming that he's missing?'

'What do *you* think has happened to him?'

'I don't think anything has happened. I think he's stayed here, sulked, and moped about, before finally accepting that I've left him for good. Then he packed up his stuff and moved on. It's all I ever wanted for either of us. He's gone and he's not coming back.'

'It's strange though, isn't it. That nobody has heard from him. No emails, texts, calls. Absolutely nothing.'

'I can't answer for that. I haven't been here.'

'Which leads nicely to my next question. Where have you been for the past three years?'

'Bardsey. I was staying in a property that one of my friends own.'

'Hmm. And you didn't see or speak with Eric the whole time that you were there?'

'Nope.' I shrug. 'Not a peep.'

'Can you explain then why his car was picked up on ANPR not far from that location in December?'

'No, Detective Inspector, I cannot.'

'Is it reasonable to assume that your husband found out where you were and decided to come and speak with you?'

'Of course, it's reasonable. But it didn't happen.'

'Are you absolutely certain about that?'

'Detective Inspector Shuter, I can categorically confirm that my husband did not turn up in Bardsey *just* to have a cosy little chat with me. I started a new life there, albeit a temporary one. I just wanted the dust to settle before I came back home and rebuilt my life.'

'Three years is a long time isn't it?'

'I suppose it depends on how you're measuring it.'

'How do you mean?'

'Three years isn't a long time when you're trying to heal

from a marriage that you thought was forever. Three years isn't a long time when you're emotionally bruised. Three years isn't a long time when your soul hurts from the very person who was supposed to be your protector. Our marriage was not a good one Detective Inspective, and I needed time.'

'Was your husband a violent man, Jade?'

Shaking my head I move from the sofa and stand in front of my bookcase, 'Eric was many things, but violent is not word enough to describe him.'

'You know, Jade...' he smiles, as he moves to stand beside me, '...the law is far more sympathetic these days concerning domestic violence. Speak to me, I can help you. If something happened, something that maybe you didn't mean to happen...'

'Nothing happened. Eric is gone. I don't know where.'

'Jade, I can help you...'

'Why do I need help? You're making assumptions now that I've done something to him. My husband is 6ft 3, I'm only 5ft 2, I think even you can work out the issues that would arise there.'

'You'd be surprised at what I've seen.'

'Actually, I don't think that I would.'

Moving across to the balcony he takes in the

spectacular views before him. The sea is a little rough today, but there are still people out on the beach, making the best of all that Whitby has to offer – even on a chilly spring afternoon. We're a hardy bunch.

'It's a nice place that you've got here, stunning view, must have cost a pretty penny.'

'Yes.' I respond, with a shrug, deciding that the less I say at this point the better.

'Mind if I take a look around?'

'Is that really necessary? I'm not hiding my husband in a wardrobe.'

'I'm sure you're not.' He mumbles as he pushes open the door to the spare bedroom and takes a peek inside.

'Why then? Why do you need to look around? Do you think I've done something to him? Something, *un-wifely*?'

'It's all just standard procedure.' He smiles again as he closes the door and moves on to my bedroom.

'Does standard procedure involve rifling through my drawers? Don't you need a warrant for that?'

'Do I need to get a warrant?'

'Oh, you're one of those.' I sigh, 'figures.'

'One of what?'

'One of those people that answers questions with a question. I'm sorry that you're wasting your time here with me – as you can see, Eric isn't here – I doubt he has been for a long time. I don't know what to tell you that will make you believe me.'

'What makes you think I don't believe you?'

Smiling, I open all of the wardrobe doors, fling open the bathroom door and the cupboards, ensuring in my dramatics that I avoid lingering too long in the spare bedroom, in particular the stuff that is bagged up beneath the bed. Eric's stuff. Stuff that shouldn't be here if he'd left me.

'Everything makes me think that you don't believe me. I've watched enough true crime documentaries to know that the police always suspect the spouse or partner first, but as you can see, there is nobody in this house but you and me. Trust me, Eric most certainly isn't here.'

'Then where is he Jade?'

'He's gone, detective – our *union* is over.'

Twenty-One

Heidi as predicted went nuclear!

'You were supposed to call me! I'm your wingman, your best friend, your bloody…bloody…sidekick!'

'We're not Batman and Robin.' I laugh as Heidi throws herself dramatically onto my sofa. 'Bloody sidekick! Look, he wasn't here long, and it would have looked shady as hell if I'd called you mid-interrogation, so…'

'He *interrogated* you?' She fumes, as she starts pacing again. 'No, that's bang out of order! We need to get you legal representation, like yesterday!'

'It wasn't really an interrogation. He was just doing his job, asking questions. I don't think I said anything that would lead him to believe I'm a ruthless killer.'

'You don't *think* you did? Jesus, Jade! Right, kettle on, then I want you to tell me word for word what you said to that copper! Word for word!'

'Heidi, I…'

'Word for bloody word! Jade, you're my best friend, my sister, I love you… but right now you need to listen to me. If that detective caught even a slight whiff that you were lying then he's going to be back and it won't be for a cosy chat and a cuppa this time. So, kettle on, and then word for word!'

Thankfully Heidi is on the same page as me and doesn't believe that I said anything detrimental to my freedom.
However, she was a little concerned that I referred to Eric as being violent, as she believes this could look like a motive. She's right, of course, and I knew as soon as I said the words that I shouldn't have. But it's scary being questioned by the police, and it's incredibly frustrating trying to keep all of that anger in when they have no idea what that monster did to me.
But still, I should have kept my mouth shut and feigned ignorance. *'No officer, I don't know where he is.'*

I haven't heard from Detective Shuter, not a peep, but I know that doesn't mean anything. He could be building a damning case against me right now and I wouldn't know a damn thing about it until I was arrested.

I have tried to walk back into my life, I have tried to pick up all of the pieces and start again, but somebody is determined to stop me and there's not a damned thing I can do about it.

I don't know who they are. I don't know where they

are. But they seem to know an awful lot about me.

I dread the sound of the letterbox. I hate knowing that I am being watched. I am in essence a prisoner of a crazed letter writer whose only agenda is to destroy me.

Twenty-Two

Pannett Park is a peaceful place and not too far away from my home, so it's the ideal location to try and get my thoughts into some kind of order.

It's quiet here today, and as I wander across to the Lily Pond to sit on the little bench opposite, I am hit with such an overwhelming sense of desolation that it takes my breath away. I have all of this, right here at my fingertips, this beauty, this peace, this solace, it's always been mine, it's always been here, and yet one man was able to snatch it all away from me. And he continues to do so.

I have always loved Pannett Park, The Commemorative Garden, The Floral Clock and the Jurassic Garden, but I have not sat here, just been present in the moment, surrounded by this beauty for far too long.

Eric took this from me, and if I am caught, if the police finally uncover the truth, then he will have taken it from me all over again. How can one man do that? How can one man have so much power over a person?

I've screwed up, I know I have. I should have called the police when Eric was killed. I could have explained what had happened. Even if they hadn't believed me, even if Jake had pinned it all on me at least I wouldn't be fearing for my life and my freedom. I could have faced whatever punishment was dished out, served my time and then moved on with my life. But I did none of those things. I listened to Jake, I covered it up, I became an accessory to Eric's murder, and then not too long after became a murderer myself. I have most certainly screwed up.

Of all of the things that I have endured, of all of the beatings, the abuse, the rapes, the insults – losing Whitby again will be the worst. Losing Whitby again will be the end of me.

13th April 2026

F.A.O Jade Sawyer

Do you wonder who I am?
How I know your darkest secrets?
Do you lie awake at night desperately trying to work out who is behind these letters and why they are sending them?

Are you scared?
You should be!

Keep a lookout for the news, I believe the next report is all about wells. You like wells, don't you, Jade?

Twenty-Three

There hasn't been anything on the news.

Have they been found?

How much time do I have left?

Are they still in there? Undiscovered? Rotting away?

Should I check?

I know that I'm trying to convince myself that going back to the well is a good idea, that checking that they are actually in there is of the utmost importance – but I have a hundred good reasons why I absolutely shouldn't – and being caught red-handed at the actual crime scene is at the top of that list.

I will not go back to the well.

I will not.

It's a problem isn't it, when you start lying to yourself.

Twenty-Four

The summer house is quiet.

No forensic tents, police cars or miserable caffeine-deprived, chain-smoking detectives anywhere to be seen.

But that doesn't mean anything does it?

All of the action could be happening in the woods – so I should avoid the woods, shouldn't I? Of course I should.

But I need to know.

The woods are eerily silent as I make my way towards the well. I'm surprised that I can remember the way to go, considering the state that I was in the last time I was here. But unlike that last time, I am unburdened by the dead weight of Jake's body. The only thing that weighs heavy on me now is what I will find when I reach my destination.

Will I be faced with an active crime scene? Will I find CSI combing the area for clues, sniffer dogs ambling around in the bushes, reporters and television crews for the local news detailing this horrific find – or will I, as I suspect, considering how quiet it is, find myself alone, facing once again the hideous realisation of all that occurred here.

The ground is damp as I trudge as unobtrusively as I can through the thicket, mulch and fallen leaves, trying as best as I can to not leave any obvious trails or footprints.

It's difficult, I muse, as I pull my hair from a gnarled branch that seems intent on snaring me, to not leave traces of yourself at a crime scene. This one piece of hair could be all it takes to '*crack the case.*'

Can you imagine… everything that I've done, all the lies that I've told… brought to light by one snagged hair.

Unless the bodies have already been found and unless the police have someone undercover watching me right now, then I'm as certain as I can be that I am alone and that nothing has been unearthed as yet.

Still, I feel as though I am not alone.

It's like the trees overhead are closing in on me, sucking out the light, ready to hold me accountable for all that I've done. All that they have witnessed.

Like the souls of Eric and Jake are watching my every move, ready to drag me into the deep dark depths of the well, where I will spend eternity paralysed and afraid under their watchful, penetrating, malevolent gaze.

Laughing nervously, I shake my head and whisper that

I'm just being stupid. Of course, their souls aren't here getting ready to pounce. I am alone. So very alone, and as the well appears ahead of me, I can't help but falter.

Am I ready for this?

Leaning over the rim of the well, I gag as an overwhelming stench of decay assaults my nostrils. It's like nothing that I've ever smelt before, and as my stomach heaves I try my hardest not to vomit.

Surely they must still be down there.

Would it smell so bad if they weren't?

I know that I can't take the lack of police presence as confirmation that they are indeed exactly where I left them, and it will play on my mind if I don't do this properly. But am I really ready to face what lies at the bottom of this deep, dark hole?

Am I ready to face what I did?

The well is at least twenty feet deep, but I came prepared, unwilling to leave anything to chance, and as I wrap string securely around my mobile phone, switch on the torch and then video mode, I pray that it holds.

Short of climbing in myself, which would be impossible at this depth, videoing the crime scene is my only option.

The other option of course would be to go home, forget

this foolish venture and face the wrath of Heidi – but I can't. I need to know, and regardless of whether I go ahead with this or not, I will face Heidi's frustration anyway. So I may as well jump right in.

Not in a literal sense of course.

I brought enough string to adequately support my phone, leaving a length of around seventeen or eighteen feet to play with, so I know as soon as that runs out I'm as far down as I'm willing to go. I don't know if the well still has water in it, it's much too deep and much too dark to tell, so I'll just have to hope that it's dry.

Covering my face with my scarf to mask the overpowering smell rising up from the well, I dangle the phone over the edge and begin to slowly lower it down– trying my best to stop it from spinning. I don't need long – just enough time to reach the end of the string, a few moments of recording and then I can get the hell out of here. Get back home, where I'm safe.

But I need to take my time. I can't rush this. I can't risk anything going wrong. If I lose focus I could very well drop my phone into this bloody well and that will be that. Game over.

Time seems to slow as my senses go into overdrive. The sound of the wind in the trees, the rustling of the leaves on the woodland floor and the slight pitter-patter of raindrops make me feel as though someone is out there, watching, waiting. Their approach masked by the blood pounding in my ears and my heart beating as though it may implode at any moment.

Breathe.

It feels like an eternity has passed when my phone suddenly comes to a halt, the string taught, unable to go any further. With a gasp, I take a moment just to steady my thoughts. Have I found them? Are they really still in there?

Pulling the phone back up just a few inches I peer over the edge. I can't see anything, not even a glimmer of the torchlight, despite knowing that it's on.

Allowing myself just a few more moments of recording time, I hold my breath as the stench of the well overwhelms my senses. I just need to make sure that I've captured as much as I can – because I am not doing this again. This is my only chance.

Slowly pulling the phone from the well with trembling hands I shut off the torch and the video and thrust the phone deep into my pocket. I won't watch it here. I can't. I need privacy and at least four Gin and Tonics before I press play on the carnage that I have recorded.

Again and not for the last time I'm sure – I just want to go home.

Twenty-Five

I may be a little drunk.

The four Gin and Tonics that I promised myself, turned into six, with a side of Vodka shots.

I have picked up my phone so many times to watch the video and then panicked, unable to press play. So, I drank and then drank some more, and when that wasn't enough, I launched the bloody thing across the room, where it now lays, mocking me with its shiny black screen.

Downing one more shot, I stumble across the room to scoop up the offending article, wobbling as I do so and collapsing onto the floor. 'Well.' I slur, 'this is as good a place as any – might as well just get on with it.'

Pressing play, I watch as my phone makes its unsteady descent into the well, the torchlight casting shadows that highlight the moss and mildew growing on the inner wall, and I feel slightly sick with the motion.

Part of me wants to fast forward to nearer the end, whereas the other part has no such desire to rush.

Lower now, I jump as the phone suddenly stops spinning, pulling me out of the daze that I was slowly sinking into. And then I recoil in disgust as I watch the phone being slowly lifted a few inches, revealing, as it spins once more, little snapshots of horror.

Unable to tear my eyes away from the screen, I try and fail to make out who is who, but it's impossible to distinguish which face belongs to Eric and which face belongs to Jake, such is the decomposition.

There is some water in the bottom of the well, not much, but enough to come halfway up the bodies of the two men that lay atop one another – men that I cannot tell apart.

Nature has not wasted its time in the five months they have been in the well, and as the phone spins again I retch, as I see maggots wriggling through the swollen flesh of Eric and Jake, eyeballs protruding from sockets, bloated mottled green skin with strange dark lines upon it, and worst of all, teeth bared as the flesh has been eaten away from their lips, their faces frozen in a rictus of pure hatred, as their screams went unheard.

Dropping the phone, I half run, half crawl to the bathroom, only just making it, as everything that I have idiotically drunk makes a hasty reappearance.

I don't know what I expected.

I don't know what I thought I would see.

But it is worse than I could possibly have imagined.

Twenty-Six

I have avoided Heidi's persistent telephone calls and text messages for the past three days, because in truth, seeing the aftermath of what I have done, well, I don't know how I can face nice, normal people ever again.

But, in true Heidi fashion, she too is a determined little so-and-so, and now as she pounds on my front door, shouting all sorts of obscenities, I know that I have no choice but to let her in, even if it is to spare the blushes of my neighbours.

'Oh, about bloody time too!' She fumes, as she pulls off her coat and hugs me, 'I thought you were dead!'

'Dead?' I squeak.

'Well, maybe not dead, but something equally horrible.'

'Is there anything equal to death?'

'Yeah! Your best friend ignoring you! Why've you been screening my calls? Where the hell have you been?'

'I… erm…'

'Oh great! Are you having a glitch again? Do you need to reboot? Honestly, Jade, I worry about you. Well, your brain at the very least.'

'You want tea?'

'Do I want tea? Do I want a bloody cup of tea? No, I want to know where you've been for the past three days?!' Picking up my phone she heads straight for my text messages and frowns. 'So you have read my messages then? Didn't fancy replying? Even when I asked if you were still alive? Nope? Didn't fancy that at all, eh?'

'I'm sorry, I've just been… busy.'

'Oh, busy! Right. Well, this should be good – busy doing what?'

Sinking down onto the sofa, I pull my legs beneath me, and shudder, 'I don't know if I can tell you.'

'*You can't tell me*? Not too long-ago Jade you told me that you chucked two blokes down a well – what could be worse than that?'

'The actual well.'

'Sorry, what?'

'Don't get mad, okay.' I smile, anxiously, as I grab my phone from her. 'Just, don't get mad.'

'What have you done?'

Pressing play on the video, I pass the phone back to a confused-looking Heidi.

'Jade, what is this?'

'Just watch, please?'

As the video plays on, I watch as Heidi's confusion is taken over by disgust, shock and then finally, as predicted, anger.

'What! The! Hell! Is! This?!'

'It's…'

'You went back to the well? You filmed *this*? Why Jade?' she cries. 'Why? Are you insane?'

'I needed to know, okay! I needed to know that they were still in there! I needed to know how much time I have left! I had no choice!'

'You had no choice?! Jesus Christ! Of course you had a choice! You stay away from the scene of the murder – that's your choice! You don't incriminate yourself any further – that's your choice! You don't film the goddamn corpses – that's your choice! Tell me, honestly Jade, what did you think you were going to get from doing this? So they're still in there, big deal! Don't you think you'll know when they're found? Don't you think that copper will be round here banging on your door with some nice shiny bracelets if they thought you had anything to do with it? Don't tell me you had no choice, Jade!'

'You don't understand!' I snap, as I grab the phone from her hand, 'nobody understands.'

'You're right there!' She snaps back. 'And you went

alone, *again*! What am I, Jade? Your best friend when it suits?'

'Oh, so we're back at that are we? Pissed because I hid the bodies without you, pissed because I went back to the well, then pissed because I went back to the well *without you!*

'You're damn right I'm pissed! You should never have gone! But if you were so determined and pigheaded about going, which you evidently were, then I would have come with you! Why do you do this? Why?'

'What? Protect you?'

'It isn't me that needs protecting, Jade.' She sighs. Sliding next to me on the sofa, she holds me as big fat tears roll down my face. 'Just promise me, if you ever plan on doing something else this dumb, that you'll let me know, okay? I can't help you if you shut me out.'

'I just needed to know.'

'Right, and now you do. So you need to delete that video.'

'I will.'

'Now Jade. Do it now, while I'm here.'

Pressing delete on the recording, I feel nothing.

If only my past could be wiped clean as easily.

'Done.' I sigh, as I show her the empty space in my camera roll where the video had been. It's funny really –

my camera roll, not the video. It used to be full of nights out and drunken poses – most of which we barely remembered the following morning – and now, it holds nothing but an empty space where a horror video was filmed. This was supposed to be my new start, new memories, new life. But absolutely bugger all has changed. Because *I* haven't let it change.

'Right. She smiles. 'Now that we know that Eric is looking the best that he's ever looked....' She sniggers, '...and the evidence of your little day trip is forever deleted, I'll make the tea and then I can tell you my news.'

'You have news?'

'Duh! It's why I've been trying to reach you. While you've been off thinking you're Lara Croft – *literal Tomb Raider* – I've been speaking with Eric's folks. They saw the news report, and wanted to know if it's true, that he's missing.'

'Why is that news?' I shrug, 'They hate him, why do they even care?'

'Because, dipshit, they want to keep Amber updated, so the poor lass can come out of hiding. And, my thoughts are this... bear with me. *If*, and I do mean *if*, the police do find out you helped dispose of Eric's body and that you then killed Jake, we might just be able to get Amber and Eric's parents on side to confirm what a monster he was, which would only strengthen the fact you were acting in self-defence. You see...?'

'Why would they do that?'

'Well, we don't know that they would. But it's worth taking note of. Anyway, I explained that yes, he is *allegedly* missing and you haven't seen him in years. They were shocked of course, but overall they seemed happy.'

'They might have disowned him because of what he did to Amber, but he's still their son. Will they feel nothing when they find out how he died?'

'I don't think they'll care. He was a bully, Jade, as you very well know. He was a horrible, evil bully. I think deep down, even though they will never admit it out loud, they will be glad that he's gone. Only the best gruesome murder for their *little angel.*'

'But what of Amber? Why would she want to help? Why would she want to put herself through the agony of telling a room full of strangers what he did to her? She has a new life now – she doesn't need this.'

'For my best friend, you better believe she's gonna spill her guts! We might just need her Jade. We might need her to push through the pain just one more time.'

'It will be hard on her.' I sigh. 'So very hard.'

'It will be much harder on me losing you though.' She frowns. 'If all of this goes tits up…'

'Heids…'

'Hey.' She grins, now. 'It may not even come to this anyway. But, if it does, she better start talking.'

'We can't force her to relive this. I can't ask her to do this for me.'

'That's why you've got me, and I'll keep on asking until the end of time, if that's what it takes.'

'Please don't push her too hard.' I beg. 'She's been through enough. This will be a big ask on her part.'

'I'm going to do whatever it takes to stop you from spending a lifetime in prison, and if that means Amber has to spend a few minutes talking about a dead man, then so be it.'

Twenty-Seven

The beach isn't as deserted as I expected it to be, which in some small way is a relief – at least I am not totally alone.

The sea is rough today as rain clouds gather overhead, and despite the chill in the air, I woke this morning thinking only one think – I want to go paddling.

Pulling off my boots and socks I run towards the icy cold North Sea, squealing as the tide hits my toes, freezing them in an instant. I know that I must look insane to the other people on the beach – the dog walkers and fossil hunters, but I don't care. I promised myself that I would do this, and looking crazy isn't going to stop me.

Heidi was right, I muse as I squelch sand between my toes. I shouldn't have gone back to the well. I need to stop living in the past. If it does indeed catch up with me, well, I'll deal with it as and when.

I need to stop acting so recklessly. Yes, I'm guilty, but I'm also a survivor. A survivor who deserves her life back.

Eric had to go, whereas Jake was purely collateral damage. I regret Jake's death, of course I do, but I can't bring him back – I am way past the point of that now.

I promised myself that I would live my best life and so far I have done anything but that.

'You're brave.' A man laughs behind me, as he throws a stick for his dog that is running in and out of the waves. 'Braver than me, that's for sure.'

'Oh, I don't know about that.' I chuckle, 'I think I'm regretting it now; I can't feel my toes.'

'Is that the only thing you regret Jade?'

Spinning around, I notice immediately that the man and his dog have walked further up the beach, leaving Ben in his place. 'Surely there must be something else that you regret?'

'Ben, what a surprise. Still stalking me I see.'

'I said, didn't I, that I'd be watching you.'

Making my way clumsily from the sea edge, I pull on my socks and boots, not caring that my feet are soaking wet and covered in a fine layer of gritty sand. I cannot stay on this beach alone with this man.

'What do you want Ben?' I ask wearily as I move to walk around him, noticing that the beach suddenly seems all at once deserted.

'I came to tell you my news. Do you want to hear it?'

'Not really, no.'

Laughing, he moves closer to me, 'I had a feeling you'd

say that. But I'll tell you anyway. I did an interview a few days ago with a reporter, Verity Cobain I think her name was. Anyway, she was sniffing about, asking all sorts of questions about Eric, *and you*. You want to know what I told her?'

'What Ben? What did you tell her? Your crazy conspiracy theory that I've somehow made Eric disappear into thin air? That I am somehow responsible for him vanishing? I don't care what you told her, and I don't care about you and your ridiculous interview.'

'Oh, you should care, Jade.' He snarls. 'You see, I didn't mention you. Well, other than to say you're Eric's wife. But, all that could change.'

'Evidently cashing in on your mate's disappearance Ben, just how low can you get? It's pathetic!'

'You're not listening Jade. I haven't told this reporter anything about *you*.'

'So?'

'So, aren't you in the least bit concerned that I will? Do you really want a journalist delving into your life, unearthing all of your deep dark secrets?'

'What do you want Ben? Obviously, you have something on your mind – as small as it is.'

'I could tell her, couldn't I, all about your marriage, the

nasty accusations you've made – that aren't backed up with any actual proof by the way. I could tell her, couldn't I, how you suddenly upped and left, not a word to anyone – and then suddenly your husband is missing. Don't you think Jade, that a journalist would find that odd? That maybe that journalist might want to look a little closer at you? That maybe that journalist might think you had something to hide?'

'So why haven't you told her any of that? If you're so sure that I'm guilty?'

'Because.' He smirks as he thrusts his face into mine, his breath a mixture of stale beer and decay, 'I thought maybe we could come to some sort of *arrangement*. I protect you, and you, well, I think you know what I want.'

I tremble with a fear I know all too well, as his hand reaches up and touches my face, and I slowly back away from him. 'You're insane! I would rather drown myself in this very sea than let you anywhere near me! Tell her Ben. Tell her whatever you want. But don't you ever touch me again!'

'You will regret this Jade.' He shouts from behind me as I run for the ramp that will take me away from him. 'You mark my words, Jade. You will regret this!'

Running blindly now as icy cold rain pelts my face, I pull my hood closer around my head, trying to hold back tears and catch my breath as I run past the amusement arcades and *The Magpie café*, dodging people and dogs as best as I can, before finally, unable to run any further I collapse against the railings of the swing bridge.

The swing bridge!

It seems no matter how hard I try; I am always running. But this bridge, this very bridge was both my saviour and my captor.

Passers-by glance down at me as they make their way across the bridge, some look concerned, others amused. Look at the crazy woman, shivering and snivelling on the cold damp floor. They have no idea.

Why am I always the one that is ignored? Why doesn't anybody ever try to help? Is that what we are in this world – just selfish, ignorant individuals who care only for themselves?

Little shadows that float around in our own little worlds?

I know of course that that is unfair.

I never ask for help either.

How can anyone help you if you don't admit you need help? If you don't ask?

But Ben's kind of help? No thanks.

'Jade? Jesus Jade, what's happened?'

I know immediately who it is. His aftershave has remained the same over the many years that I have known him, and as his strong arms envelop me and pull me to my feet, I continue to avoid the curious stares of passers-by and sink into Gordon's chest.

'Jade?'

'I...'

'Can you walk?' He asks, concern etched across his handsome face, 'Jade?'

Nodding, I pull away from the warmth of his body, feeling all at once bereft and cold. 'I think so.' However, placing one foot in front of the other seems to be a task that now evades me, and as I fall forward, I am once again caught in his arms.

'Well...' he chuckles, as he scoops me up, 'I'll take that as a no. We need to get you warmed up... home?'

Shaking my head, I tell him no, not there, trying to ignore the look of confusion that flashes across his face. Pulling me closer he marches across the swing bridge and into *The Dolphin*, and I know that I am going to have to explain why for the first time in a long time I don't want to go home. And I haven't a clue where to start.

As Gordon places a hot chocolate in front of me, I wrap my hands around the cup, grateful for the warmth, but already missing the heat from Gordon's body.

I don't know what to do with these feelings that I have for him. Feelings that have seemingly come out of nowhere. He's always saving me, I know that. Maybe that's it. Maybe they're not romantic feelings at all, maybe they're just… oh, I don't know… gratitude?

'Penny for them?' he laughs now, as he sips his coffee and eyeballs me. 'You were miles away.'

Smiling back, I take a long gulp of my hot chocolate, fully aware that not even for one million pounds would I ever tell him what I was just thinking.

'What are you doing here?' I smile.

'Just looking at some property.' He grins.

'Oh, because you don't have enough already?' I laugh. 'Just how big is this portfolio of yours?'

'Well, that's a leading question if ever I heard one.'

'You're always saving me; do you know that?' I sniff.

'Well, that's what friends do, isn't it?'

Friends.

'Yeah. I suppose so. But I've not saved you once.'

'You wanna tell me what all that was about?'

'Ben was at the beach. He collared me.'

'He what?!' Gordon's rage is instant as I try my hardest to calm him down. 'What did he do? Did he hurt you?'

'No, no. He was just banging on about some reporter that he's done an interview with. He was talking crazy.'

'Reporter? Why would he tell you that?'

'Because she's looking into Eric's disappearance.'

'So he's really missing then? Well let's hope she doesn't look too hard – we don't need him back! You would tell me though, wouldn't you, if there was something else bothering you. I might be able to help.'

Sobbing, I take another sip of my drink, my hands shaking as I place the cup back down on the table. 'I wish that I could. I wish that I could tell you everything. But I need you to trust me, okay. I can't tell you. It's not because I don't want to, it's because I don't want you to get hurt. Do you understand?'

Scooting closer to me, he takes my shaking hands in his as he shakes his head, 'I don't understand a damn thing, Jade. I need you to help me understand.'

'I can't.'

'You can! Do you know how hard it was for me to find out what that bastard did to you? Do you? You should have come to me; I would have helped you!'

'I know how hard it was Gordon.' I snap, 'because I was

bloody there!'

Pulling me to him, he holds me as close as he can and kisses my forehead. 'I'm sorry. I am so sorry.'

Pulling away just a little, I look into Gordon's eyes. 'I'm sorry too.'

The kiss that follows comes totally out of the blue.

I was not anticipating it, I was not planning it, and I am most certainly not rejecting it.

As his lips find mine, they are gentle and soft, but also so incredibly fiery hot. Pulling him closer I feel his hands in my hair, my hands in his, our bodies melting together as a passion neither one of us envisaged suddenly becomes all-consuming.

A kiss like no other.

What the hell am I doing?!

Pulling away from him, I can barely catch my breath as I see the heat in Gordon's eyes, no doubt mirrored in my own. A heat that has no right being here, right now, or ever!

'I'm sorry.' I whisper as I move away from him, 'That shouldn't have happened.'

'Shouldn't it?' He whispers back, as his lips seek mine once more. 'I'm not complaining.'

'I'll only hurt you.' I cry as I make a dash for the door.

'I'm sorry, I really am.'

'Jade, wait!'

Ignoring him, I rush up the cobbled street, passing the *White Horse and Griffin*, not caring who sees me now, past the bookshop and into my house in record time.

What the hell was I thinking?

I can't do this... this... whatever the hell *this* is, with Gordon!

He's my best friend's brother!

I am a murderer!

No matter what feelings I have for Gordon. Feelings that I do not have any space in my life to consider right now – I cannot lead him on. I cannot allow him to believe that we have a chance. *Yeah, a snowball-in-hell kind of a chance!* The second he finds out what I've done, he will hate me.

Even if he didn't hate me – which is a big if – how could I live with that? Knowing that his perfect reputation could be damaged – because of me!

Imagine, we get together, all is nice and rosy, and then BAM, I'm arrested and sent to prison – for a very, very, very long time – how can I expect him to deal with that? How can I expect him to stand by me?

No.

I may have feelings for Gordon and he may have feelings

for me. But we *can't* work. It's impossible. It's damaged before it's even started.

I won't do that to him.

I won't do that to me.

Twenty-Eight

Work has not been easy today. I wanted to avoid it. I wanted to call in sick and hide away until all of this blows over, but it won't will it? Not until the police have discovered the truth.

Mr. Timmons was understandably full of questions as were some of the locals:

'Am I okay?'

'Do I need to take some time off?'

'Where do I think Eric is?'

'Are the police any closer to finding him?'

'Did he leave a note?'

'Do the police think it's suspicious?'

'Is anyone else involved?'

I shook my head at each question, carefully avoiding words that might incriminate me. I'm sure I looked utterly hopeless, weak, and pathetic, but that's what I need everyone to believe, isn't it? That I'm the concerned, confused, troubled wife? And I am concerned, I am troubled, but not over him. Never over him.

BODIES FOUND IN DISUSED WELL LEAVE INVESTIGATORS BAFFLED

Whitby News   Monday 27th April 2026
By: Verity Cobain – News Reporter for the Whitby News

As the hunt for missing Accountant Eric Sawyer ramps up, it can now be reported that two bodies have been found in a disused well in East Keswick.

The two males are at present unidentified and there is nothing to suggest at this point that they are in any way linked to missing man Eric Sawyer of Whitby, North Yorkshire.

Police have again asked that anyone with any information, regarding either Mr Sawyer or the two unidentified men contact them as a matter of urgency.

Verity Cobain – News Reporter for the Whitby News.

Twenty-Nine

'Calm down. Okay, so they've found the bodies – it does not mean that they have any evidence that points to you.'

The second that I saw the newspaper in the shop, I felt faint. Then I felt sick to the stomach with worry, prompting Mr. Timmons to call Heidi and send me home for the day, with a cheery wave and a *'don't come back until you're better.'*

And now, as I sit on my sofa with my head in my hands I can't think of one single way that this could ever be better!

'I'm screwed!'

'No, you're not! They've not even identified them yet. We've seen the video Jade, trust me, that's going to take some time.'

'And when they do?'

'Then you put on the performance of a lifetime. Shed a few tears, wring your hands, pace the room, throw up! This is not the time to go to pieces.'

'Well, when is a good time?' I scream. 'When I'm being taken away in handcuffs?'

'We can only deal with what we have in front of us. Right

now we know that two bodies have been found. Two *unidentified* bodies. You cleaned the house, you left no trace of yourself there or at the crime scene, you deleted the video – they have nothing but two decomposed corpses.'

'What if I didn't clean it enough? What if I left traces of something at the well? They're professionals, we're not.'

'Yeah, they're professionals with not an awful lot to work with. Even you couldn't tell the difference between Eric and Jake, and you knew them better than anyone.'

'If I confess now, they might go easier on me.' I suggest as I move to switch the kettle on. 'If I tell them what Eric did to me…'

'No! Absolutely not! You need to act as clueless as possible about all of this. As far as you're concerned, your marriage didn't work out, you left him, and that is it!'

'And what about Jake? I'll have to fess up about that relationship at some point.'

'What relationship? You had a few dates, it didn't work out, you came back home to ask Eric for a divorce and he was gone.'

'Sounds a bit far-fetched doesn't it?'

'It isn't your job to find the links, Jade, it's theirs, and any that they find will be tenuous at best! They need evidence – and they don't have any.'

30th April 2026

F.A.O Jade Sawyer

Do you remember the night that two men were murdered?
Do you?
Of course you do. The aftermath of your crime is all over the newspapers – I wonder who pointed the police in that direction?
Do you recall the wind, the rain, the utter devastation?
You didn't see me.
But I saw you.
I saw what you did and then I watched you walk away.
You walked away!
How could you do that?
People need to know what you did.
*They will know what **you** did!*

Thirty

It would appear that not only have I angered my best friend a lot recently, but now, also my therapist!

Are care providers allowed to be mad at you?

Doesn't that go against everything that they stand for? Well, regardless of what I think, Stella is most certainly mad at me.

I suppose it doesn't help that I've also now confessed that I've been lying to her since the moment that we met.

No, no… I haven't told her *everything*!

Just my real name and a reasonable explanation as to why I lied – running from an abusive ex-husband, going into hiding, starting a new life – that kind of thing. She was of course sympathetic, until she frowned and said we'd need to start from scratch now.

Why have I decided to be partially honest with Stella? Because I'm exhausted, that's why. I'm sick and tired of being Peyton Grey. My name is Jade Locke.

I AM Jade Locke!

I have also made a decision about my future. Well, I'm considering it anyway. I just need to clarify a few things with Stella first. No longer do I feel the need to spill my guts to this woman. She isn't the right person to help me; I know that now. She's much too happy clappy with her letter burning and *'how do you feel?'* questions. But, I do need her professional opinion on the thoughts that darken my every waking moment, despite knowing that her responses will push me towards what my frazzled mind has already deduced.

The only person that can help me, is me.

I've told her about the letters. Not the letters that I've been receiving, especially not about the most recent one, the one that is sure to damn me – but the letters she made me write, and that did not go down well either. I think maybe Stella should see someone. She has some issues with patience I think.

'The whole point of the exercise was to write the letters and then burn them... Jade.' She glowers at me over the rim of her spectacles. 'It was the *main* point!'

'I'm not ready to do that.' I argue back, 'I might want to add something else.'

'Then you write another letter and burn that too.'

'Seems like an awful lot of letters and fire, don't you think?'

'Miss Gray... erm, Jade... It doesn't matter how many

letters you write, so long as you burn them immediately afterwards. To help you heal.'

'Honestly, it's going to take more than burning a few letters to help me heal.'

'How do you know that? You haven't burnt one yet!'

See what I mean… no patience!

'Do you think that now that you've told me a little more of the truth about yourself, you might be able to embellish on that a little more?'

'I don't think I'm ready to talk about any of that just yet.' I sigh. 'I don't even know where I'd start unravelling such a mess.'

'Right.' She smiles, *impatiently*. 'Why don't we start by discussing what has brought you here today?'

Standing, I begin to slowly pace the floor in front of her huge desk, 'I've done something stupid. Something that might be the end of me.'

'Can you tell me what you've done?'

'I went somewhere that I shouldn't have gone. Somewhere from my past. It was dangerous and reckless, and so bloody stupid!'

'Why shouldn't you have gone there?'

'Because if anyone knew what I'd done and why I'd gone back there I'd be in a whole heap of trouble.'

'Jade…' she frowns, 'I can't help you if I don't know what you've done, or what kind of trouble you're in.'

'I'm not in any trouble. Yet.'

'But you believe you will be in trouble?'

'Oh yes. The worst trouble anyone could possibly be in.'

'Look, why don't you sit down, take a moment, and then tell me exactly what it is that you are scared of?'

'I'm scared of living.' I sob as I drop like a rock into the chair by the window. 'I'm scared that I can't live with what I have done.'

'And what *have* you done? You know, I can't help you if I don't have a least some small idea of what you're going through. Are you in trouble with the police?'

Snorting, I pull the yellow cushion from behind me and pull it onto my lap, 'you could say that.'

'And does this trouble involve your ex-husband?'

'In more ways than one.' I frown, as I push the cushion to the floor, feeling restless now. 'Is everything I say in this room totally confidential? Like you couldn't call the police if I told you something really bad?'

'These meetings are confidential, yes.'

'But?'

'But… in some extreme circumstances, I would have a duty to break that confidentiality.'

'What classes as an *extreme* circumstance?'

'It's not really as black and white as that, I'm afraid. I suppose to give a brief example, if I felt you were a danger to yourself or to others then that would give me cause to think about breaking that confidentiality.'

'But not a past crime? You wouldn't call the police if you were told about something that had already happened?'

'It really would depend on what that crime was.'

'Murder.'

It's interesting watching how the word *murder* resonates with people. Take Heidi for example, she was shocked and then she was annoyed that I hadn't asked her for help. But at no point was she scared.

However, Stella White looks petrified.

'Murder?' She squeaks. 'Jade, I…'

'Would you report murder to the police? Would you break patient/doctor confidentially if it was about a murder?'

'Are we talking hypothetically here Jade? Have you witnessed a murder? Taken part in something that you now regret? If either of those are the case here, then I would urge you to speak with the police. Have you been involved in something, Jade?'

Shaking my head, I reach down and scoop up the yellow cushion, placing it perfectly on the chair behind me, before squashing it up and leaving it crumpled.

'Maybe. Maybe not. How can I answer that now when I don't know what you will do with the information?'

'Jade… If you have something to confess, something that you need to get off your chest, well, I'd like to remind you that this *is* a safe space.'

Opening the door now, I take one last look around Stella's immaculate office, bar the crumpled cushion of course and smile, sadly. 'I have plenty to confess. But not to you.'

IDENTIFIED REMAINS OF TWO MEN LEAVE POLICE WITH MORE QUESTIONS THAN ANSWERS

Whitby News   Saturday 9th May 2026
By: Verity Cobain – News Reporter for the Whitby News

Whitby News can today confirm that the remains of two men found on private property in a disused well in East Keswick are that of Mr Eric Sawyer, 34, and Mr Jake Walker, 32.

Their family and friends have been informed and have requested privacy during this difficult period while they come to terms with this tragic discovery.

Verity Cobain – News Reporter for the Whitby News.

Thirty-One

It takes a lot of courage I think to admit when you are wrong. To accept that you must face the consequences of your actions. To put yourself in a position where you are vulnerable, no longer responsible for your own life, your own decisions, your own wellbeing.

A position I already know too well. But this time, for totally different reasons.

It takes a lot of courage I think, to face the truth.

I hadn't walked out of the therapist's office with a fierce determination to set things straight. One plan, one path, one final destination. I had instead headed immediately home and drunk myself into oblivion.

I had switched off my phone, closed the curtains and drunk and drunk and drunk until the realisation of all that I have done, all that I have encountered, suffered, put up with and survived was nothing but a hazy blur in my spinning head.

I hadn't made any plans, written any speeches, or made any excuses – I just simply drank until I could drink no more.

The following day I showered, made the bed, emptied the

dishwasher and the bins, and sat in silence.

My mind was clear. My mind was made up.

I wrote long open and honest letters to both my parents, Heidi, and Gordon, and I got dressed.

I emptied pills onto the coffee table, and I stared at them, for what seemed like hours. Lots of little white pills.

A way out.

A simple yet effective way out.

Then I read a book, drank a cup of tea, and placed the letters on the coffee table, next to the pills.

A way out.

I know in my own mind, in my own heart that I will be caught. Of course I will. I'd be stupid to think otherwise.

Between the bodies of Eric and Jake being found, Ben and my mystery letter writer, there isn't any other way that this could play out.

Do I deserve to suffer for the murder of my husband?

I don't think so. I'm glad that he's dead.

But Jake?

I think Jake's death was a turning point for me. Maybe not in the heat of the moment, but in every moment since.

And so I look once more at those little white pills.

A way out.

Thirty-Two

I hadn't taken the overdose – it had seemed, in the end, like a cowardly thing to do. And despite how dreadful things would be for my family and my friends once the news broke that I had been arrested, I acknowledged that finding my dead body would have been a whole lot worse.

After sobering up and throwing the pills away, I had sat down and really thought about what I'd done, and how realistic it would be for me to A) get away with it, and, B) live with it.

Neither had good results.

Which only left me with one of a few possible answers:

1) Go on the run.

2) Live a sad sort of non-existence.

3) Take the overdose.

4) Confess to everything and take my punishment.

Number four won out in the end, and as I stood outside of the police station, with no idea what was to come next, I felt a strange sort of peace. I felt calm.

I cannot live my life hiding away, scared of the letter box rattling, scared of my own shadow. I know that the police won't go any easier on me because I have decided to come forward. I know that I won't get a lesser sentence. But I will get one up on my mystery letter writer.

Thirty-Three

Pushing open the door of the police station, I am immediately faced with a desk, protected by a Perspex screen and a rather busy-looking police officer rifling through some papers. It almost seems a shame to interrupt him, but interrupt him I must.

'Excuse me.'

'Just a minute love.' The police officer responds without looking up, 'I'll be right with you.'

'You look like you've done summat really bad.' A raspy voice croaks from behind me, 'like butter wouldn't melt.'

'Shut up Darren.' Hisses the police officer. 'You're the one that's in bother, not her. Can I help you love?' He smiles at me now, his missing papers all but forgotten.

'I need to report a crime, please.'

'See! Told ya!' Darren laughs. 'Butter wouldn't melt!'

'Shut it! I won't tell you again! Ignore him,' He grins. 'He's heading for yet another stretch, aren't you Daz?!'

'Screw you, man.' He sulks, as he folds his arms across his chest and turns to face the wall.

'Right, so what's this crime? Someone nicked your purse?'

Taking a deep breath I lean closer to the Perspex window.

'Murder, officer. I've killed someone.'

'Come again?'

'Bloody told ya! Murderer! Butter wouldn't bloody melt!'

'Shut up Darren, for crying out loud!'

'Officer...' I start again but with more force this time, '...I have *murdered* somebody, I would like to *confess*, and I would like to do that *right now* please, if you wouldn't mind.'

'Who have you murdered, Miss...?'

'Locke, my name is Jade Locke, formerly Jade Sawyer. If you look at that newspaper behind you, you'll have some idea of who I am.'

Picking up the paper he scans the news report quickly and then stares at me, 'The accountant? What about him?'

'My name was Jade *Sawyer*.' I begin slowly, 'The man in the paper is Eric *Sawyer*, my ex-husband.'

'So, you're here to ask about the investigation?'

'No.' I take a steadying breath, 'I'm here to confess to the murder of the man that was found in the well with him. Jake Walker.'

'Did you kill your husband, Mrs Sawyer?'

'It's Miss Locke, on account of him being dead, until death do us part and all that. And no, I didn't. Just Jake.'

'Oh, just Jake.' He frowns, 'Well that makes it alright then!'

'I never said that it was alright.'

'Careful.' Darren butts in, 'she'll be killing you next!'

'Can I please speak with Detective Inspector Shuter?'

'Oh, known are you?'

'No, I am not *known*. But he's already questioned me about the disappearance of my husband, so I know his name from that visit. Look, I get this is a small police station, and maybe murderers don't walk in here off the street as a rule, but shouldn't you be taking this a little more seriously?'

'Just take a seat will you, while I call DI Shuter. He doesn't like being disturbed, so if this is some kind of prank…'

'I can assure you; it isn't.'

It's a crazy flurry of activity once Detective Inspector Shuter makes his way downstairs to the reception area. As I am ushered into a chilly interview room, I am overcome with the sudden reality of my situation. There's no going back now. I have willingly confessed to murder.

'Miss Locke? Or is it okay if I call you Jade?' DI Shuter asks with a friendly smile.

'Jade is fine.' I respond, not returning the smile.

'Jade, I'm somewhat confused, so maybe you can help me out here. The last time we spoke you were adamant that you had no idea where your husband was. And now you walk in here confessing to a murder. But not that of your husband. What am I missing here?'

'Detective Inspector, I lied to you the last time we spoke. I knew exactly where Eric was, I've always known, and I'm very sorry for deceiving you.'

'Ah, well.' He begins, as he twiddles his pen around his fingers, 'I knew you were lying Jade, I just didn't know about what. You see, the way I figure it, your husband was violent, so you left him, then in a moment of madness you decided to come back and kill him – am I right?'

Shaking my head I lean back in my chair and close my eyes. 'My husband wasn't violent, he was evil. The things he did to me, I couldn't even begin to put into words. The abuse, the mind games, the humiliation. My husband was a monster, but I didn't kill him.'

'Then who did, Jade? Who killed him?'

Opening my eyes, I sigh, 'Jake Walker killed him, to protect me.'

'But you said you killed Mr Walker? Why would you do that if he was your protector?'

'When you've suffered the way that I have, when you've had your freedom taken away from you, when you've suffered pain like no other pain you've ever felt, then and only then could you possibly understand why I killed Jake.'

'I'm going to need a lot more than that, Jade! Why did you kill Jake Walker?'

'Because he was going to take everything away from me! Because he was just like Eric, because he wouldn't let me be free!' I snap. 'I just wanted to go home!'

'Well, I hate to be the bearer of bad news Miss Locke, but if what you've said is true, you won't be going home for a long time. So let's try again, how did Eric Sawyer, your husband end up in a well with Jake Walker? From the start, Jade.'

And so, I explain.

My marriage, running away, how Eric tracked me down, Jake helping me to escape, and finally, the night that inevitably sealed my fate. I tell him everything.

'I killed Jake, detective, but I did not kill my husband.'

'That's going to be a little tricky to confirm though isn't it – considering you murdered the man that allegedly did? Seems too neat for me, Jade, I'll admit. It was your husband you wanted dead, and yet you didn't kill him. But some poor guy who has the hots for you meets a sticky end instead. You have to admit, it doesn't sound good.'

'I don't care what it sounds like. I didn't kill Eric.'

'Can't prove it though, can you?'

'And neither can you.'

'Why did you come here today?'

'What?'

'Why now? Was it the news that prompted this visit? Did you know it was only a matter of time before I came knocking on your door again?'

'How could I know that? Yes, I saw the papers, but that wasn't why I came. I came because I killed a man. I came because my guilt was unbearable.'

'I don't believe you. I think you knew once we found the bodies that we would immediately look at you.'

'Why would I think that?'

'Because they both had their wallets in their pockets, Jade.'

'What?' I'm lost for words as DI Shuter produces photographs of the evidence found in the well, and sure enough there are two driving licences staring right back at me. Eric's and Jake's. I hadn't even considered that they had their wallets on them. Why would I?

'I think you remembered the wallets and you panicked.

Figured if you confessed before we had to come and arrest you, you'd get off lighter. Does that sound about right?'

'No. No that isn't true! I didn't know about the wallets. I didn't. I wasn't exactly thinking straight that night!'

'Ah, yes, the night that you bludgeoned two men to death and dragged their bodies to a disused well, leaving them there to rot.'

'One man! I only killed one man!'

'Only?'

'You're twisting my words!'

'Do you know what a body looks like after five months in a well, Jade? Would you like to see? I have the photographs right here.'

I can't admit that I've already seen what they look like, he'll really go after me then. Call me a psychopath, heading back to the crime scene to admire my handiwork

'No.' I squeak. 'No.'

'Maybe later then. Tell me, Jade, after you killed… we'll just say Jake for now, what did you do? Head right back home? Make up for lost time?'

'I'll never make up that time.'

'C'mon, humour me.' He smiles, again, 'you go out with the girls, maybe treat yourself to fish and chips? What did you do?'

Has he been following me?

'Yes, I went out with my friends. I also saw a therapist. I'm not a ruthless killer Detective, I'm just a normal woman who wants a normal life.'

'The evidence would say otherwise.'

'What evidence?' I ask, genuinely intrigued. 'What evidence do you have other than my confession?'

'We have two dead men that were known to you, Jade! We have an abusive husband, a jilted lover and we have you!'

'But that isn't evidence, is it? That's just a peculiar coincidence. All you have is two dead men, their wallets, and their names. Sure, I was married to one and briefly dating the other, which you'd find out in the course of your investigation – but what *actual* hard evidence do you have? Without my confession, it's all circumstantial.'

'It's a good job I have that then isn't it?' He bawls as his fist hits the desk.

'But you don't. Not really.'

'How's that then?'

'Well, everything that I've just said hasn't been recorded. I think that's because you didn't believe me when I first came in, or maybe you're just tired and forgot to turn on the machine, I don't know. But right now, you don't have any evidence that I just confessed to murder. So, that's no physical evidence and no confession either, detective. Oh, and you didn't read me my rights.'

'Think you're clever, don't you?'

'Not at all detective, I'm merely pointing out the facts.'

'I can still hold you for twenty-four hours, Jade.'

'And then what? You let me go and continue with an investigation that won't ever produce any tangible evidence? Detective Inspector Shuter, I need you to believe me when I tell you that I only killed one man – Jake Walker. I did not kill my husband. I need you to believe me, otherwise, after twenty-four hours I'm going to walk free. You'll have let a murderer walk free.'

'And what makes you think that I won't find any evidence against you?'

'Because I didn't leave any.'

'You sure about that?'

'I am.' I smile. 'I wasn't before I came here, not really. It gave me a lot of sleepless nights in fact. But I know for certain now that I didn't.'

'So why continue this charade? If you don't believe that I'll find anything, why carry on?'

'Because I murdered a man, detective. You're not listening to me. I killed Jake Walker. Me. I did that. I need to face the consequences of what I did. I can't live any kind of life otherwise. Also, I've told you what I've done. So regardless of whether or not you release me, you will always be searching for proof, and I can't live my life like that either.'

'You're telling me, that despite zero evidence against you and now no taped confession, you still want to go ahead with being charged with murder? Is that it?'

'Now you're listening.' I smile. 'But only for the murder of Jake. I will confess all over again to the murder of Jake Walker, but I will not confess to the murder of Eric Sawyer, because I didn't do it.'

'That's going to be a little difficult to prove.'

'For you it is. So, shall we do this properly… with the tape on this time?'

LOCAL WOMAN ARRESTED OVER THE BRUTAL SLAYING OF TWO MEN

Whitby News   Wednesday 13th May 2026
By: Verity Cobain – News Reporter

A shop assistant who is alleged to have stabbed her lover to death after helping him to dispose of the body of her husband has today been arrested.

Jade Sawyer (formerly Locke), 33, of Henrietta Street, Whitby, North Yorkshire, has been remanded into custody to appear at Leeds Crown Court following the death of her husband, Eric Sawyer, 34, and lover, Jake Walker, 32.

Police were initially contacted by concerned friends of Mr Sawyer and then received an anonymous telephone call with detailed information on where the bodies were hidden. Police are urging the individual who made that call to come forward and help further with their enquiries.

No further statements have been made by the police regarding the arrest at this time.

Verity Cobain – News Reporter for the Whitby News.

Thirty-Four

It's been two weeks since my confession and subsequent arrest. Despite everything that I said, I have been charged with the murders of both Eric and Jake and will stand trial sometime in August.

I'm sure a lot of people will wonder why I played things the way that I did in the police station. I had after all quickly established that they had no proof that I had been involved at all. But I couldn't continue to live a lie any longer. It was tearing me apart. I would eventually have cracked, and those little white pills would most certainly have held a lot more appeal.

Prison is not at all like the TV shows that I've seen. It's scary and intimidating and already I've been threatened twice, just for looking at someone the wrong way, apparently. I'll have to watch my back for the remainder of my time in here – which could be a while if I'm charged with Eric's death also.

My cellmate is an elderly lady called Pauline, she's in for a double murder too – which she fervently denies. I haven't asked her for any further details, because it's not the *done* thing in prison, as I've quickly learnt. I had assumed from the telly that inmates wore their crimes like a badge of honour, but it's simply not true.

My barrister, a tall, skinny man called Miles Crispin, is adamant that he can get me off the murder charge where Eric is concerned, but has told me quite frankly that due to my spoken and written confession, the murder charge pertaining to Jake will more than likely stick, and I'll be looking at a sentence of around fourteen years – though he'll do his best regarding that.

I had of course balked at fourteen years – how would I survive fourteen years in this hell hole?
Yes, I could have walked away, but I had thought, somewhat naively that maybe I'd get ten years, a little less for good behaviour – but fourteen years!
Haven't I lost enough years already!

Visiting time at the prison is a stressful day.

You would think that it would be nice, that the prisoners would be happy, for a moment at least. But it's the exact opposite. For those inmates that don't receive visitors, well, they make damn sure you feel like shit for receiving yours. You dare not smile; you dare not look remotely pleased – you just act as though it's a normal, never-ending day of nothingness. Which prison ultimately is.

However, today, I can't help the bubble of excitement that is floating around in my chest, because mum and Heidi are coming to visit.

I'll admit, I'm nervous. It's the first time that I've seen either of them since I was remanded – though I have spoken to them briefly on the phone.

Mum had of course been in utter turmoil when she heard the news, and I had spent the whole of that initial phone call calming her down and telling her that I was fine. I was perfectly fine. Dad blamed himself. And poor Heidi has been left to pick up the pieces again in my absence.

It's been difficult for everyone involved.

I haven't heard from Gordon, though in truth, our budding romance, or blip, or whatever it was, isn't something that I can dwell on right now. Not because I don't have time – believe me, I have plenty of that, but because it's something else that I have intrinsically ruined. I just hope that one day he can forgive me.

As the buzzer sounds there is a scurry of feet as we all make our way into the visitor's room. It's nothing fancy, just a plain blue room with chairs and tables that are bolted to the floor – but we haven't come in here to admire the appalling décor, we have come in here to see the faces of those who are determined to stand by us, no matter how tough it gets on the outside.

Rushing forward I instantly see mum and Heidi and relief floods through me that they actually came. I can see them with my own eyes, hear them with my own ears, and briefly touch them before the prison guards tell me to move away. They are a vision of pure light – and the only thing that will get me through the many dark days that are yet to come.

Taking our seats, we all begin to talk at once, laughing as our words become entwined, forming a jumble of incoherent noise. It's mum who breaks the awkward laughter.

'Oh, Jade, love.' She sobs. 'You've lost a lot of weight – are they not feeding you properly. I've seen these shows before you know, on the television, these prison dramas – is someone stealing your food, I can…'

'Mum, mum.' I soothe. 'Nobody is stealing my food. It's just a lot to get adjusted to that's all. How's dad?'

'Not himself.' She sighs. 'He won't be happy until you're out of this place.'

'It might be a while yet, but my barrister is working on it. Once we've been to court; we'll have a better idea of what we're looking at.'

'Yeah, well he better pull his finger out!' Heidi fumes as she wipes away a tear, 'I need you. Why did you do this Jade, why?'

'I already told you. I needed to. For me. Look it won't be forever. Before you know it we'll be back at *The Dirty Rabbit*, singing shitty duets and crawling home.'

'Hey, our duets were not shitty!'

'They were a little shitty.' I laugh.

'Nicky and Jess send their love – and weirdly, Barry too! Everyone is behind you. And those that aren't... well they better stay away from me!'

'Thanks Heids.'

'That reporter has been sniffing around – almost every day now.' Mum interrupts, 'I was thinking I might call the police, get some kind of restraining order. We've had to unplug the house phone.'

'Who's this?'

'That Verity Cobain from *The Whitby News*. Hounding us she is, for a story.'

'Isn't she the one that Ben did the interview with?'

'Nah, it was all bollocks – sorry Mrs Locke.' She apologises to my mum. 'It was all utter *nonsense*. I called her out on it, asked when she'd be printing that tossers –

Sorry, that... *man's* interview – she said she had no idea what I was talking about.'

'I don't know why I'm even surprised.' I sigh, 'It's just lie, after lie, after lie.'

'Should I call the police about her then?' Mum continues, 'It's harassment, surely.'

'I don't think they'd do anything. If she's on a public street and not your actual property, then...'

'Well, that's just ridiculous.' Mum fumes, as though that's my biggest concern right now.

'Oh, before I forget.' Heidi begins, 'Gordon asked me to pass on a message. He said he's sorry that he hasn't been to visit, but he's not sure he could handle seeing you in here without making some kind of attempt at breaking you out.' She laughs. 'And then randomly – he said I've to remind you about the book?'

'The book?' I ask, confused, before it hits me. *The* book!

'That mean anything to you?'

'Yeah.' I smile, sadly. 'Tell him thanks, will you. Tell him that I often think about it.'

'Okaaay! You two are weird. So what's it like in here?' Heidi asks as she cautiously looks around the room, 'are you even safe?'

I know it's a big deal for Heidi to be in prison, and I know that her cheeriness is all a front, so I appreciate her visit more than anyone else's. After what Ethan put her through it's hardly surprising that she wouldn't want to be here. But as my best friend, she's really putting her all into getting me through this. I just hope it isn't damaging for her.

Ethan is not a nice person.

Oh, he's good-looking enough, probably too good-looking actually. But to be handsome and charming as well as a monster underneath is a lethal combination. Heidi was suckered in by Ethan and his charismatic charm. On paper, he was a winning lottery ticket, but in reality, he was the numbers that you always used religiously, until one day you decided to switch it up, leaving you missing out on the million-pound jackpot.

He never laid a finger on Heidi, which is just as well for him, as Gordon would have pulverised him. No. Ethan was manipulative in other ways. He bullied Heidi, and what Ethan wanted, she provided, such were her feelings for him. Ethan is a career criminal, you see, used to getting his own way, used to calling the shots. When Ethan spoke, everyone listened or suffered the consequences.

However, it all came to a head for Heidi when he asked her to deliver a *parcel* for him. She wasn't stupid. She knew what was in it and she flat out refused to be involved. That is where their *relationship* ended.

Ethan had made his fortune in the drugs game. All class A, all deadly, and it finally caught up with him.

Ethan wasn't caught out because Heidi grassed on him though. Ethan was caught out because he thought he was untouchable. I can only presume at this point, that he feels a little less untouchable, as he sees out his eight-year vacation in HMRC Armley.

The reason Heidi doesn't like prisons isn't because he's currently in one. It's because had she been caught with that parcel on that day, then she would probably be in one too. Heidi would hate prison even more than I do.

Now, in response to Heidi's question, '*are you even safe?*' Well, had mum not been here, I would have told her that I don't feel remotely safe. I barely sleep, and barely eat, I hate the communal showers and the toilet that is on display. I hate being stared at, threatened, bullied. But most of all I hate that my family are suffering along with me. I hate that I am putting them through this.

But I don't say any of those things. Instead, I shrug, smile as best as I can, and tell her I will be fine.

'I'll try and get your dad to come with us next time – he's just a little sad right now, you understand? But he loves you, we all love you.'

'Can you tell him that I love him too and that he doesn't need to come here. I'm not hurt that he's not here mum, I'm hurt because I've put you all through this and now I'm in here and can't do a bloody thing to help you! But I'm not angry, or sad that he hasn't come. Please tell him that I understand.'

As the buzzer sounds, indicating that visiting time is over, I want nothing more than to walk out of those doors with them. To feel the sun on my face, to sleep in my own bed, to hold everyone and tell them not to worry about me. But as they turn to leave, I know that those things will not be possible for a long time.

August looms, and along with it, my fate.

Thirty-Five

'**O**i, Sawyer!' A voice booms from behind me. 'You've got a visitor.'

Dumping my tray of, well, I'm not quite sure, I follow the prison guard out towards the visitors' room, eager to see who has come to see me. It's probably my barrister, and I'm hoping he has a plan that involves me not spending the next fourteen years of my life with split personality Pauline.

I'm right, it is Miles, and as I sit opposite him I note instantly that he looks a little cheery.

'I hope that smile means you have some good news?'

'Possibly.' He grins as he reaches inside his rather expensive-looking leather briefcase.

'Well…?' I urge.'

'You remember the day you left Whitby?'

'Like it was yesterday.'

'Well, I have two witnesses ready to testify that on that day you looked half out of your mind with fright.'

'Eh? You do?'

'I do. Do you by any chance recall speaking to a Mr.

Graham Barley on that day?'

'Who?'

'He said he bumped into you at the bottom of the 199 steps, the day that you left Eric'

'Yes! Yes, I do. But I never got his name. Why would he help me?'

'Well, he's been following the news and immediately recognised you. He made a call to my office and I've been out to see him.'

'I don't understand. It was hardly a full-blown conversation. It was less than brief, at best.'

'He recalls feeling worried about you. He said that there was just something he couldn't put his finger on, and then when he saw the news he put two and two together. You see, his sister went through something similar. He was only a boy at the time, but he told me that thinking back he should have known that you were running away. What with the suitcase and the desperation in your voice…'

'How could he know any of that? We barely spoke.'

'Because, in his words, he said, '*I've seen that haunted look too many times to count*'. So he's more than prepared to testify to that.'

'But that's not going to be enough, is it? A look on my

face? A brief chat with a stranger? The prosecution team will trample all over it.'

'That's very true.' He continues to smile.

'Then why are you smiling?' I snap.

'Because his testimony alongside that of Betsy Brown will…'

'Who the hell is Betsy Brown?' I interrupt. Totally fed up now with this nonsense.

'Only the woman that helped you get on the bus to Leeds.'

'Oh god, I'd forgotten all about her.'

'Well, she hadn't forgotten about you. She was another one who recognised you on the news. She didn't hesitate to call. She told a compelling tale about you being chased and the state you were in.'

'She was lovely.' I smile, remembering how much she helped me. She even gave me her telephone number before I got on the bus, and I had forgotten all about her. 'Is it enough though? Is it enough to get me off killing Eric?'

'It's a start. We need to prove loss of control. Something triggered by the violence that you had suffered for so many years at the hands of your husband. If we can get the jurors to understand just how desperate you were to get away from your husband, how you feared for your life, only to be faced with a man showing similar traits as him, who then went on to murder your husband, then we can show that not only were you fearing serious violence from Mr Walker but that this final event triggered your PTSD causing loss of control.'

'I don't have a formal diagnosis of PTSD.' I sigh.

'But you will have, once you've seen the doctor that has been approved by both the Judge and the prosecution team.'

'Oh. Oh, well, okay. I guess that's good then.'

'You'll be seeing him tomorrow morning.'

'What do I say? What if I mess up?'

'You won't mess up, just be honest.'

'Do you think the jurors will believe me?'

'We'll see, Jade. We'll see.'

Whilst Miles's response isn't exactly encouraging, I know that it's not his job to placate me. He doesn't have a crystal ball; he can't read minds. He's in the dark just as much as I am when it comes to the jurors. I haven't lied once about what Eric did to me, but maybe, just maybe I'll have to up the drama and give them an even darker description of the violence that I suffered. Maybe then they will understand.

As I stand to leave, I feel Miles's hand touch my shoulder ever so gently. 'There is one more thing Jade.'

'Oh?'

'We have Amber.'

Turning to face Miles, I smile sadly. 'Why would she help me? Why would she put herself through this again?'

'Because, your friend Heidi put quite the argument to her, that's why.' He grins, confidently. 'Amber has confirmed more than once that she'd be happy to take the stand in your defence.'

'Oh, Miles.' I sigh, as I walk back towards the prison guard and back towards my lonely cell. 'I'll believe it when I see it. I'll believe it when I see her.'

I will not get my hopes up.

I will not.

Doctor Cahill has a friendly face. Slightly weathered looking, but friendly. I don't know what I was expecting, but Doctor Cahill isn't it.

The room that we have been allocated for the examination or test, or whatever the hell it is, is not particularly fancy, so the prison governors clearly have no grand designs to impress the Doctor. But then I don't suppose he cares much for being impressed. I'm just another patient on another day and this is just his job.

'Mrs Sawyer.' He begins, as he unpacks a notebook

and pen from his bag. 'I don't want you to worry at all about this test, the questions are standard and...'

'What kind of questions are they? Do I need to tell you everything that happened?'

'All you need to do is answer the questions in your own words and then I'll take it from there.'

'So it's like a point-scoring exercise?'

'Precisely.'

'Do I get more points for being a murderer?'

Ignoring me, he flips his notebook to a new page and asks if I'm ready to start. I nod that I am, even though truthfully I would rather be anywhere but here, being tested on my worthiness to have PTSD.

'Mrs Sawyer, do you often avoid places that are associated with trauma?'

'Please could you call me Jade? Is that okay?'

'Yes, certainly.' He smiles. 'So, do you, Jade?'

'That's a tricky one to answer, as the majority of what happened was in my home and I still live there. So it's difficult to avoid.'

'Do you find it difficult being at home?'

'I did when I first came back. The memories in that house were overwhelming. But I just try my best to deal with them, to not think about them.'

'Do you ever suffer from nightmares or flashbacks?'

'I do, yes.'

'Have you ever been in what *you believed* to be an emotionally abusive relationship?'

'Yes. Eric was both emotionally abusive and physically abusive. I didn't *believe* I was in it. I *was* in it.'

'Have you experienced sexual and physical abuse?'

'Yes.'

'Have you developed any unhealthy behaviours, such as drinking or substance abuse? Or eating disorders?'

'I was drinking a little more than usual I suppose, but I've always been a bit of a drinker, you know, when I'm out with friends.'

'But do you find yourself drinking alone a lot more?'

'No. I had one day where I was drunk in my house on my own, but it was only the once.'

'And how did that make you feel?'

'Pretty stupid when I sobered up.' I smile, 'It's sad isn't it, drinking alone?'

'At the time, did you believe the abuse was your fault?'

'At the start I did. I thought it was my behaviour that was winding Eric up, that I was doing things wrong just to push his buttons.'

'And were you?'

'What kind of question is that? Of course I wasn't! He was insane. It was him! He was the one making up new rules all of the time, rules that I couldn't ever possibly adhere to. He was crazy.'

'Did you stay in the relationship because you thought he would change?'

'I hoped he would in the beginning. But then the violence escalated and I knew that he never would. I didn't want to stay in my marriage, but he made it impossible for me to leave. I was also for a time wheelchair bound, so that didn't really help.'

'Have you ever felt your sense of self-worth was lost? That you no longer recognised yourself?'

'All of the time. But that's what they do, isn't it? They beat you down until you don't have a clue who you are anymore. They have all of the power.'

'Do you feel like he has any power over you now?'

'No.'

'And why is that?'

'Because he's dead.'

'And yet you suffer nightmares and flashbacks, so do you think maybe he does still, to some degree, control your emotions?'

'He's dead doctor, he'll never control me again.'

Thirty-Six

The door to my cell is unlocked every morning at 06.45AM, but I'm usually awake long before then because it's damn near impossible to sleep in this place. There are so many sounds, cries of innocence, rage, threats and gentle sobbing that echo around the cell walls during the night, that even if I could sleep it would be out of the question.

I've tried to plug my ears with toilet roll, cover my head with my flat pillow, and stick my fingers in my ears, but nothing works. The sounds, the chaos, it just filters through, like an earworm played on a loop. However, I don't make any noise. No matter how much I want to scream and shout and make threats of my own if the crying doesn't stop. I do nothing. I just lay in silence, praying it will end. I also don't want to make any enemies.

I've tried my hardest to stay away from the other prisoners, which is a little tricky in such a confined space. Mostly I succeed – until breakfast time arrives, at least. It's then, that we must all queue up together under the watchful eye of the prison guards, all hoping that it isn't something horrible on the menu. It's always something horrible.

Pauline, my cellmate is the only person that I speak to. The other inmates tend to leave her alone – whether it's because of her age or the fact that she's a bit mad I'm not really sure, but she seems nice enough. Well, as nice as you can be in here.

I have a little job now, cleaning the kitchen, which is okay. Sometimes I get put on laundry duty which I hate as some of the women here are unbelievably unhygienic. I know that we are in prison, and I know that not one single one of us has anyone to impress, but still, letting yourself go as some of these women have done is just sad.

Sometimes when I lay in bed on a night on the most uncomfortable mattress imaginable, I think of Whitby. I think of the beach, the view from my house, of watching the storm clouds roll in. But mostly I think of the peace. A peace that I might not know again for some time.

I miss Whitby.

I miss my family and my friends.

I miss the sea.

I have received letters of support since being here, and some letters of pure hatred. I keep them all, as a reminder of all that I have done and all that I have survived.

However, I have not received a single letter from my mystery letter writer, so I suppose they must be happy now, as justice is very much on its way to being served. I do wonder though, what they must be thinking now? They will have no doubt watched the news and read the papers religiously since my arrest. Are they sitting comfortably at home, happy in the knowledge that they *brought me down?*

Are they keeping a scrapbook of their victory? Something to look back on when they need a laugh?

Their conquest clippings! Their success stories!

I should imagine that they will be delighted that I am to be punished – and that's fine by me. I do deserve it. For Jake at least. But I hope, I really do hope, that as they follow my trial, they can understand, in some small way, why I did what I did. But maybe, in reality, they just don't care. They did after all just stand by and watch as I disposed of Jake's body. If they were so concerned about what I'd done, then why didn't they try to stop me? Why didn't they try to help Jake?

I guess my letter writer isn't as innocent in all of this as they believe themselves to be.

Thirty-Seven

I always thought that courtrooms looked quite cosy on the television – everyone huddled together, telling a story - but in real life, when you're sitting there, preparing to be judged, it's as intimidating as hell.

I am brought in through a side door, my head low as I feel burning shame flood my cheeks. It wouldn't be so bad if I were just allowed to walk in. But I am instead escorted to the dock by a big, burly security officer, who never smiles, never speaks to me, and who enjoys giving my handcuffs a little tug, just to ensure that I haven't mastered lock picking in the past three minutes. I am officially a criminal now. The shiny handcuffs prove it.

The Judge – His Honour Judge Rupert Bartholomew-Smythe KC, has already done his opening speech, and the jury has been called in. A portly man with red cheeks and white hair, Judge Bartholomew-Smythe has a friendly face, but he also looks like the kind of man that will not allow any nonsense in his courtroom.

The public gallery is full, with my friends, my mum and dad, the press - and Ben! I should have known that he would be here, and as I catch his eye, he grins at me, a look of *'I knew it'* written all over his smug little face. Gordon is not here.

As the prosecuting barrister, Callum Jones, begins his opening statement, I wince as I am described as a ruthless killer, a woman with no remorse for what she has done, a calculated murderer responsible for the manipulation and brutal slaying of two innocent men. Evil personified.

And then it's my barrister, Miles Crispin, detailing the abuse that I suffered at the hands of my husband, the fear I felt for my life, the horror of my every waking moment – 'Mrs Sawyer is not a ruthless killer, she is not manipulative or calculating, she is just a normal woman who fell in love with the wrong man, a man that she *did not* harm, despite the countless number of times that *he* harmed her. Mrs Sawyer does *not* deserve a hefty prison sentence. Mrs Sawyer did *not* kill her husband. However, she did confess to the murder of one Mr Jake Walker, and *that* is the only crime on trial here.'

Naturally, the prosecution team were not going to leave that hanging, and as I am called to the witness box, to swear under oath that I promise to tell the truth, the whole truth, and nothing but the truth, I am a bundle of nerves.

'Isn't it true, Mrs Sawyer, that on the day of December 3rd two thousand twenty-five, you hatched a plan so cunning and barbaric that by the end of that very day, two men would lay dead, by your hand?'

And so the trial begins.

A trial that will either condemn me or free me. I think I know which outcome I will put my money on.

Thirty-Eight

I answer every question with absolute clarity. I do not lie. I do not leave anything out. I do not try and make myself look better for the jury, and I do not weep as one by one my friends and my parents are interrogated.

Of course, mum and dad don't know anything, they can only tell the court what I told them, which is minimal, to say the least. I feel dreadful as I watch my parents being questioned, as the truth of what I have done is revealed and the impact it immediately has on them.

Their daughter, the killer.

My dad, oh my dad, the hurt in his eyes as he looks across the courtroom at me. Not disappointment, not judgement, not anger – just hurt. Hurt, that I didn't tell him, hurt, that I felt I couldn't.

I feel nothing. Nothing but shame.

One by one every single person that I know is hauled in front of the judge and grilled mercilessly by the prosecuting barrister, and as each person swears to tell the truth the whole truth and nothing but the truth, I die a little inside. I brought this upon them, I made this a chapter in their lives and there is not a damn thing I can do to change it. As Nicky steps down, she gives me a little smile, a smile that I can only interpret as '*why didn't you tell me?*' And I close my heart against it. I have hurt so many people, but I can't take on their pain right now. I need to be strong. I can apologise later, and I can explain later, but right now I need to think about me, I need to think about how I'm going to survive this.

I don't see Gordon until he is walking down towards the stand. I can only assume that he had opted to wait outside until he was called to speak. He does not look at me, he stares only at the barrister as he bravely and calmly defends me, just as Heidi did. Then when he is done, he straightens his suit jacket, steps down from the box and walks right back out the door he came in.

He does not acknowledge me. He does not smile at me. He just leaves.

And on and on it goes.

The Therapist.

The woman who ran me over in December 2021.

The doctor who saved my life and the doctor who finally diagnosed me with PTSD.

Graham Barley and Betsy the bus lady.

Dorothy / Sally / Jemima.

Eric's parents.

Ben!

The list of witnesses is never-ending, and with each person that speaks I feel my freedom drifting further and further away. Some are on my side, while others condemn me further by outing my reckless drinking and dancing at *The Dirty Rabbit*, or my paddling in the sea, carefree, easy. I never saw these people, these strangers that now sit before me, judging my behaviour. How can they do that? They don't know me. The prosecution has gone all out finding randomers to dish the dirt, to speak ill of me, to make me look selfish and unrepentant.

Who are they and why are they further damaging my chances of a lenient sentence?

Sure I have the PTSD diagnosis and sure I have Betsy and Mr Barley but how does this help me when so many other people saw me acting so brazenly.

Both Betsy and Graham can say that they witnessed me fleeing, that I look haunted, scared, broken. But that's only two people against the many that the prosecution has presented. I'm grateful for them, I truly am. But if my sentence relies upon getting on a bus and a look upon my face, then I am screwed.

'Defence now calls Amber Delaney to the stand.'

Miles's voice booms out across the courtroom and I look around desperately seeking her out. I had not dared believe that she would show up. I had not let myself get my hopes up. So I tried to forget about her. I had tried to ignore the butterflies as they fluttered merrily away in my stomach, I had tried to forget that she and she alone could be the one person in this whole tragic affair that could back up my story. I had dared not believe it.

But she's here. She's really here.

I feel Ambers' fear as though it were my own. As though the look in her eyes and the pounding of her heart are mimicking mine somehow. She must be petrified sitting up there, alone, preparing to tell a room full of strangers a tale so barbaric, so inhumane that at times it will almost seem unbelievable. Fictional. Total make-believe. I know exactly how she feels because I feel it every single time I utter Eric's name.

'Miss Delaney.' Miles begins, with a smile and a nod of encouragement. 'I would like to thank you first of all for attending today, I appreciate that this won't be easy for you, and I would like to stress that if you need to stop at any point then please just let me know.'

'Thank you. I will.' She smiles back.

'Please take your time, there's no rush. But if you could start please by describing to the court your experiences with the deceased, Mr Eric Sawyer.'

'Eric was charming, sweet, kind – everything that you would want in a partner. Our life together was perfect. We even talked about marriage and having children one day.'

'You were a model at the time, is that correct?'

'I was trying to be. I'd had some good jobs, but hadn't quite made it to the modelling that I wanted to do, the modelling that I was really interested in.'

'And what kind of modelling was that?'

'I wanted to primarily work in glamour modelling.'

'And what exactly would that entail? Lingerie shoots, that kind of thing?'

'Exactly.' She sighs, as she subconsciously touches the scar on her face.

'And was Mr Sawyer supportive of this style of modelling?'

'At first, he was. He'd drive me to shoots, and hang about for hours until I was finished. He was really supportive.'

'And what changed?'

'Eric opened my post one morning while I was in the shower. He'd come to pick me up for another shoot, so he was downstairs while I was getting ready.'

'And what was in that post that he'd opened?'

'It was the images from the last shoot that I'd done.'

'The shoot that Mr Sawyer attended with you?'

'Yes, he was there the entire time.'

'What else was in the envelope?'

'A note, from the photographer, saying that I looked hot and that he would definitely be using the images.'

'What happened then?'

'Eric came rushing up the stairs, shouting about the photographer being a pervert, that he just wanted to... erm... I'm sorry, am I allowed to say exactly what he said?'

'Please do.'

'Well, he said that the photographer just wanted to fuck me and that I must have led him on for him to think that and for him to send me the note. Then he ripped up the photos and left.'

'Did you see Mr Sawyer again that day?'

'I didn't see him for a few days after that. I was in shock and I was upset, so I was happy not to see him, not until we'd both cooled down.'

'What happened the next time that you did see Mr Sawyer?'

'It was like nothing had happened. He was back to being

sweet and kind and lovely. But things had changed then, for me. I didn't want to be with a jealous man. Modelling was my passion, but it was also my job, *just* my job, there wasn't ever anything sexual about it, with either the photographers or any of the male models, it was just my job.'

'And so you had decided to end the relationship?'

'I had. But as Eric always did, he managed to talk me round, and before you knew it I had moved in with him. It was like a whirlwind.'

'And things went back to normal?'

'Yes. He was back to being the kind Eric that I knew.'

'Can you, in your own time, explain to the court what happened the night that you decided to leave Eric and what had led up to that moment?'

'Eric had been acting strange for a few weeks before our final parting. He would snap at me over silly little things, push me around and call me horrible, vile names. But the final straw came when he turned up at one of my photoshoots and caused a scene. He was swearing at the photographer, knocking things over, calling the models whores. It was humiliating, so I grabbed my things and left, without him. When he called me, I ignored him, and he called me, a lot! That night I knew he had a work meeting and that he would be out late, so I asked my friend, Carly, to help me get my stuff packed up so that I could leave him. I didn't want any further confrontation with him, so I thought going while he wasn't home was the best idea.'

'But he did come home, didn't he?'

'He did. He was steaming drunk. So when he saw what I was doing he went ballistic and attacked me. The neighbours must have heard my screaming because the police arrived. Eric was long gone by then though.'

'And what had Mr Sawyer done to you?'

'He beat me and then he slashed my face with a knife. He said that I'd never be able to model again now. The man was a psychopath.'

'And what of your friend, Carly?'

'She had tried to help me when he was hitting me, but he was like a man possessed and he punched her in the face and pushed her into the bathroom. She was too afraid then to come back out until the police arrived.'

'Did you press charges against Mr Sawyer at that point?'

'I did, but the police couldn't find him to arrest him, and that's when the stalking started.'

'Mr Sawyer had then begun stalking you?'

'Yes. I would return home and things in my house would

have been moved. Tins lined up in the cupboards, my clothes arranged in colour order. It was all very strange. I would arrive home to find my underwear, nothing else, just my underwear, had been washed and hung up to dry, and the TV would be on playing some gruesome murder documentary, it was all too much. But when I started to notice that he was following me and watching me when I was out with friends, I knew I had to do something drastic as he was never going to leave me alone. He would call and text me over and over and over – he was obsessed.'

'And yet you dropped the charges against him?'

'I did. At that time I was so frightened of him. I was still trying to come to terms with the end of my career, my face was ruined, and I was a mess. I just wanted to get as far away from him as I could. I knew that he wouldn't get a prison sentence for what he'd done to me, and even if he did, well, as soon as he was out he'd pick right back up where he left off. It wasn't enough.'

'So what did you do?'

'I spoke to Eric's parents. Explained everything that was going on and they kindly offered to help me.'

'And how did they do that?'

'I had no money, not really. I wasn't working so there wasn't anything coming in. Eric's parents helped me get set up in a new place. Somewhere Eric would never think to look for me. I stopped using bank cards and social media, I was effectively in hiding.'

'And he never found you?'

'No. I have been very careful. My life has been incredibly sheltered since escaping Eric. I haven't had a romantic relationship, I haven't made new friends, I only accept jobs that pay cash – because he was relentless. Like a shark stalking its prey. He destroyed my life.'

As Amber leaves the witness box she turns to look at me, her face a mixture of exhaustion and relief. This is over for her now. She can move back home. She can pick up the pieces of her shattered life and start to heal. I am happy for Amber. I hope that she can make a new life free of the monster that destroyed us both. But for me, the story continues. My ending has yet to be decided.

Despite Amber's incredibly brave testimony, the second that the photographic evidence is presented to the jury I really start to panic.

Before the photos, it was just people talking. It was just the juror's own imagination. But when the photographs are shown of the well, the bodies and the wounds, I know that this is what will finally sway the jury one way or another.

Never mind my testimony that I was a battered and abused wife. Never mind the horror story of my life that I told them all about in minute detail, never mind Amber's heart-wrenching tale of devastation – it means absolutely nothing at all once confronted with precise and detailed images of what I have done. The only thing the jurors will remember about this case now is the photos. The grim, hideous, disgusting photos.

Fourteen years Miles said.

It's beginning to look like he might have been wrong.

BATTERED WIFE KILLS HUSBAND AND LOVER IN SAVAGE CRIME OF PASSION

Whitby News   Saturday 8th August 2026
By: Verity Cobain – News Reporter

A 33-year-old woman murdered her lover and husband in a cold and calculated attack Leeds Crown Court has heard today.

Mrs Sawyer (formerly Locke) stated to the jury that she had suffered years of violence and emotional turmoil at the hands of her tormentor Mr Sawyer and despite trying to leave him and start a new life, he tracked her down, once again unleashing a torrent of physical and emotional abuse upon her.

Mrs Sawyer denies the allegation that she murdered her husband but did confirm to the court that she is indeed guilty of the murder of Mr Jake Walker, a revelation that has shocked many in the local community.

Mrs Sawyer stated that the incident was a 'tragedy' and that she 'deeply regrets' what happened that day.

We will of course keep you updated as this sinister tale continues to unravel.

Verity Cobain – News Reporter for the Whitby News.

Thirty-Nine

Sensing movement above me, I note that Pauline must be waking up, ready for another day of brain-numbing joy. Today is visiting day and Pauline never gets visitors, so while I'm bubbling inside with happiness, she is understandably pissy.

'Well, that was a grand night's sleep.' She groans as she creaks her way down the bunk bed ladders.

'You slept?' I ask, shocked.

'I was being sarcastic.' She snarls, 'how can you sleep in this shithole with all the loonies out there screeching.'

'Oh.' I mumble, unsure how to continue the conversation with Pauline when she's so evidently cranky today. 'I think maybe they're just stressed.'

'Stressed!' She barks as she makes her way to the toilet in the corner. 'They don't know what stress is!'

'Well, I think there's a lot to be stressed about in here.' I dare to argue.

'Oh yeah? Like what?'

'Loss of freedom, not seeing their families, not…'

'Oh, boo hoo! Cry me a river!' She snaps as she flushes

the toilet and heads to the sink. 'At least the majority of that lot out there will be out in a few years. I'm a lifer, never seeing the light of day.'

'Well, I...'

'You think pissin' and shittin' in front of strangers for years and years gets any easier? Well, it doesn't! It's as humiliating now as it was on the first day I arrived! So don't be giving me that bollocks that they're stressed! When they've been here as long as I have, then they can cry and keep us all awake!'

'Okay.' I sigh, unable to communicate any further with her. Clearly, today was not going to be a good day.

'You don't seem to have much to say for yourself this morning.' She eyeballs me, 'but then I suppose us innocent ones are really the victims, aren't we?'

Against all prison protocol, I ask Pauline if she really is innocent, or, like the others that lay awake at night screaming she's really just pissed off she was caught? I immediately regret it.

'You really asking me that?'

'I'm sorry. I don't know why I did. Please just ignore me.'

'Let me tell you something missy, I did not kill those fellas, though I should have – perverts!'

'Oh, okay.' I whisper, wishing I hadn't opened this

particular Pandora's box.

'So you wanna know, eh?'

'No, really, it's okay. It's your business. I'm sorry I asked.'

'Well since you're so interested.' She growls, 'It was my pimp and a client, who thought they could do me dirty. I disagreed.'

'You were a…'

'Whore? Yep – got a problem with that?'

'No, I…'

'I only stabbed them a little bit. I didn't kill them. I'm innocent!'

'So what did kill them?'

'Blood loss, obviously. Did you not study biology at school? The body needs blood – they had none.'

'As a result of you stabbing them?'

'You sound just like them fancy lawyers! You think I killed them, is that it? You wanna make something of it?

Obviously, I want to argue the point that they wouldn't have been bleeding had she not stabbed them, but Pauline looks manic and I'll admit to feeling terrified of her.

'No. No.' I smile. 'You're right of course. Bodies do need blood. It makes perfect sense.'

'Right then.' She grins, 'Get yourself washed and we'll

head out for brekkie.'

'What? I…'

'C'mon girlie, the best stuff will be gone.'

Shaking my head, I use the toilet, wash my hands and face and brush my teeth and walk down for breakfast with a now cheery Pauline.

What the hell just happened?'

I don't know what that was, I don't know if Pauline has some kind of mental illness, but I need to stay on her good side if we are to remain cellmates.

I worry about Pauline. Though, maybe in truth, I worry more about myself around Pauline. I do understand her point. There are a lot of women in here that pretend to be innocent. That will keep that act up for as long as it takes to get them in front of a sympathetic parole board. But Pauline? Pauline isn't acting. She truly believes that she is innocent, and that scares me almost as much as her fifteen personalities do.

I wonder if it's possible to request a new room?

Forty

Wrapping my arms around Heidi, I take a moment just to feel her warmth, the scent of her perfume, just the very realness of her. However, Heidi isn't alone, and as much as I hoped my second visitor would be Gordon, I am really pleased to see Nicky.

'Hey jailbird, how goes it?' Heidi sniggers as she gives me a squeeze. 'Master the peeing in public yet?'

'Oh, har-de-har, you are just *so* funny. As it happens, I am pretty masterful at it.'

'What? Really?'

'No! It's gross!' I shudder, 'it's even more disgusting than the witches' piss that Barry brews up.'

'Hmm, that good eh?!

'It's good to see you, Nicky.' I smile, 'you okay?'

Her silence stuns me, and as I look to Heidi for help she gives Nicky a little nudge.

'I'm sorry.' Nicky sobs as she reaches for my hands, 'I just wish…'

'That I'd told you?'

'Why didn't you? Didn't you trust me?'

'What? No! That isn't it at all.'

'Then why?'

'Because I didn't trust *him*. I didn't trust Eric. He was never going to stop looking for me. How could I have put you in harm's way like that?'

'You told Heidi.' She pouts.

'But I never intended to. Look, Nicky, I'm sorry, I am. But I was doing it to protect you. I tried to protect Heidi too, but it all just came out. I was in a bad place, I needed to get it off my chest.'

'But you..'

'I can't apologise anymore. I'm sorry if I hurt you. I'm sorry if you feel left out. But I'm in prison for murder Nicky, so as much as you feel bad, I can assure you that I feel a damn sight worse!'

'Right.' She sighs, 'I guess I'll just wait outside in the car.'

'Nicky, c'mon, this is just daft.' I plead with her. 'We don't need to fall out over this. I don't want us to fall out over this.'

'I just wish you'd told me.' She sobs, 'he hurt you and we didn't know.'

'Nobody knew. Not really. But he's gone now, he can't hurt me anymore and I need you guys. I do.'

'You're in prison because of him.'

'No. I'm in prison because of me.'

As silence falls over the table I don't quite know how to break it. What more can I say that I haven't already said?

'Ooh, I have this for you.' Heidi screeches as she reaches into her bag. 'It's from Gordon.'

'Oh.' I gulp, 'what is it?'

'It's a letter dipshit.' She laughs, 'Wow, prison has made you even more dumb.'

'A letter from Gordon?'

'You think I don't know.' She grins.

'Know what?'

'Yeah?' Nicky asks, 'know what?'

'That those two have been making googly eyes at each other. It's so obvious – Jade has a love letter!'

'What?' I stammer, 'no, it's…'

'It's a love letter – admit it.'

'It's just a letter.'

'I don't mind you know. I think you and Gordon would be pretty cute together, so…'

'There is no so…'

'Just because he's my brother…'

'Heidi! Stop! Bloody hell.'

'Are you and Gordon a thing?' Nicky asks. 'Really?'

'No.' I snap, as Heidi yelps Yes.

'They so are.' She laughs.

'Okay, change of subject. How are things on the outside? Are my mum and dad okay?'

'Erm, your mum is great, she's throwing herself into all sorts of crafty projects. She's entered the greenest lawn competition – I mean why is that even a thing?'

'And dad?'

'Who even thinks up such a stupid competition?'

'Heids? Is my dad okay?'

'Jade, he's… I don't know, heartbroken, I guess. He's quiet, that's all I can say really. He's just upset.'

'I think he's hurt because I didn't tell him what was going on. I wish I could see him, explain. But he won't come here, and well, can you blame him?'

'He'll come round Jade – he just needs time.'

'Yeah, well I have plenty of that.'

'Jess said she'll come next time. There are actually quite a few people that want to visit. You have quite the fan club.' Nicky laughs, 'even Barry said he'd pop in.'

'Yeah?'

'And we're all taking it in turns to check on your house, water your plants, a bit of dusting etcetera. It'll be like you've never been away when you get back.'

'Thank you.' I smile warmly, 'I never even thought of that stuff.'

'Which leads nicely into the next thing I need to mention.' Heidi grimaces, 'The thing is, we need to make sure that your bills are paid, and I know that you don't have everything on direct debit. So do you want me to set those up for you or do you want me to pay them at the Post Office, because if you do…'

'You'll need money. Of course. God, how could I not think of these things..'

'You've had other more pressing things on your mind, that's why.'

'I didn't bring my handbag when I turned myself in, so it should still be in the kitchen with my purse in and all my bank cards, so you can use those. If you need any passwords for the bank, and my PIN number then they're in a little pink notebook in my bedroom, top drawer of the dressing table. God, such a practical thing. I didn't even think.'

'Don't even give it another thought. I'll sort them all out.'

'What would I do without you?'

'You'd come home to a dirty, dark house with dead plants?'

'So true.' I smile, sadly. 'Any other news? Any goss?'

'Not much.' Nicky answers, 'Jess has purple hair this week, it strangely suits her.'

'Is that it? C'mon guys, just because I'm in here it doesn't mean you can't tell me the fun stuff. I want to know, I really do.'

As the buzzer sounds the end of visiting time I start to panic. I haven't asked them nearly enough. They haven't told me nearly enough. I haven't used the time wisely at all. I don't want them to go. I don't want to go back to my cell with crazy Pauline, I don't want to do this. I don't want to be alone.

As hot tears fall down my face, I crush Gordon's letter against my chest – will it be the lightness in all of this dark? Or something else to shatter me?

'You gonna open that or what?' Pauline asks from above me, 'you've been staring at it for hours, it's boring.'

'What? I....'

'Love letter is it?'

'I don't know.'

'Well, you won't unless you open it.'

'I'm scared to.'

'Stop being such a wimp.' She cackles. 'Whatever's in there can hardly be any worse than where you actually are, can it?'

'That's true. But what if it's Gordon telling me something bad? Like he doesn't want to see me ever again? I don't think I can handle that right now.'

'If that's the worst thing that you can think of then you really are stupid. Look around you. You're locked up in here with me every night, you piss and shit behind a curtain, you have no freedom, no life, you have to avoid being beaten up every day and you look like a bag of shit. How can one letter be worse than that? Just open it already!'

'But…'

'Open it. Christ, I hope I'm not stuck with you for the next twenty years, I'll go mad!'

Jade,

I hope that this letter finds its way to you.
I hope the prison guards pass it on.
I am sorry that I haven't been to visit, but if I saw you in that place if I saw you broken and hurt, it would inevitably break me. It's weak I know when you are in there dealing with it daily, but how can I be so close to the woman that I love, that deep down I have always loved and not be able to rescue her.
Yep, you heard right. I love you.
Now, if I know you as well as I think I do, then you will be panicking right about now. You'll be worried about Heidi, though I think she already suspects. You'll be worried about all that has happened and you'll be worried about the future, but mostly you'll worry that I'm Heidi's brother – It's really not that weird, don't listen to my sister!
Did I hit the nail on the head?
You don't need to worry about anything. I'm not expecting you to declare your undying love for me, I know that you have enough on your plate right now, and I will come and visit you, I promise. I just need time to prepare mentally. I just need a moment to ready myself for not attempting to break you out.
(F.A.O prison guards, that was a joke!!)

You asked me that day on the bridge why I was in Whitby. Well, as I said, I was looking at properties, just not the sort of property I'm used to looking at.
- my portfolio will be even bigger ;)
I'm working on something special, something big, and I'm hoping that you'll be here to help me with it. If not, if things don't go as planned in August, then rest assured I will have it ready for the day you walk out of that place. Ready for you.
I don't want to give anything away and Heidi will be sworn to secrecy so don't even try :) But it's special Jade.

I will see you soon, I promise.

Oh, one more thing…
PS, I Love You.

Forty-One

Prison is a strange existence when you really break it down. Obviously, it's not meant to be a home away from home or a holiday camp, I get that. We're all here to be punished, rehabilitated, and taught a lesson – but does it have to be so dull?

When I wake, if I even sleep, I use the toilet behind the curtain, aware that my cellmate can hear every single thing that I am doing, and vice versa. I have a sponge wash, brush my teeth and get dressed in my rather limited wardrobe. Some mornings I shower properly, though I try to avoid that as much as I can as it's just horrendous.

The shower room has a few cubicles for privacy, but those are mostly taken by the women that you try your hardest to avoid, which leaves only the open shower. There are seven showers in that long stretch of humiliation, and whilst I don't have the worst body of everyone in here, it is still degrading to wash yourself fully under the watchful eye of the other prisoners. So unless my hair desperately needs washing then I mostly make do with sponge washes.

I head to breakfast, which is always something awful.

Porridge that does not resemble porridge, rock-hard toast, fried eggs swimming in fat. It's dreadful, but at least it's something to do.

When breakfast is finished I start my job cleaning the kitchen with my work colleague Charlotte. She never says much, which is okay I suppose, but some conversation would be nice. When work is done I head back to my cell. I don't like to linger outside because that's where all the trouble happens. Boredom sets in quickly around here and some of the inmates like to break that up by fighting, and it's brutal. So I avoid it at all costs.

I have a little window in my cell. It's tiny – not that I was planning to escape through it considering the fifty-foot drop – but it's nice to see the weather. It isn't Whitby weather of course, no storms are rolling in, or waves crashing against the shore, but it's something.

In the afternoon we are permitted thirty minutes of fresh air and we are all hustled outside to the courtyard – again, a lot of fights break out here, so I mostly stand with my back against the wall in the furthest corner I can find. I'm sure at some point I'm going to be targeted. I'm dreading it, but it's inevitable.

The rest of the day passes by in a blur of reading, trying to sleep, and imagining all of the things that I am going to do when I am released.

A walk on the beach.
Paddling in the sea.
A long hot shower.
Food. Real food.

I know that the girls are looking after my house, but will I even be welcome back home once I'm released. If some of the vile letters that I have received are anything to go by then I reckon I'm in for a tough time on the outside also.

Nicky said that I have a lot of supporters. But what of those people that don't support me? They don't understand. They can't understand what it's like to live in constant fear. All they know is whatever is printed in the newspapers. All they hear is that someone amongst them is a cold-blooded killer. That's all they want to know.

The drama. The evil. The tragedy.

Most people love watching a crime series on the telly. They lap it up. Serial killers, wife killers, husband killers, crimes of passion – but only because it's on the telly. They don't want one of those people as their neighbour. Who would?

Gordon has made his feelings perfectly clear, which has brought some much-needed light to my life, and I wish with every fibre of my being that I could be with him. That none of this had happened, that I'd never met Eric, that Gordon and I had found each other first – but that's a fantasy, it will always just be a fantasy.

As much as I want August to arrive, I am also dreading it. I have done all that I can do in terms of pleading my innocence where Eric is concerned, and I have admitted guilt fully for Jake, so now, my future and the amount of time I spend here rests solely on the shoulders of the jurors. I hope they believe me. I pray they believe me.

Forty-Two

August 26th has come around at an alarming rate, and whilst I am somewhat relieved that the day has finally arrived, I am also incredibly frightened.

I have now served four months in prison, which doesn't sound like a long time, but when your days are filled with avoiding conflict, staring at nothing and talking to yourself, those days are insanely long. If I get the fourteen years as Miles predicts then I am going to need a better strategy to survive them.

The courtroom is once again full to bursting with my family, friends, reporters and rubberneckers. From my seat in the now very familiar dock, I watch as Miles begins frantically writing notes in his rather fancy-looking notepad, and as I try my hardest to avoid looking at anybody that I know. The urge to break free of this plastic prison is unbearable. I just want to run to my family and hold them tight. I want to sit with them while my fate is revealed. I don't want to sit here alone. But I must. I must remain composed and passive, no matter what is said about me, I must not react. I try my hardest to stay focused and not fidget. To avoid staring at the jury, my family, and my friends. But it's tricky when everyone is rehashing my life as though it were a book. Just fiction. But it wasn't fiction. It was all very real.

As the prosecution team begin their closing statement, I am once again labelled a ruthless killer, a manipulator of everyone and everything. The jury is told that I am not a victim at all, that I am an attention seeker, I am devious and sly, a pathological liar. I lack empathy and I feel no remorse whatsoever for the murders of both my husband and my lover. I am dangerous and I am guilty beyond a shadow of a doubt.

Miles does not look up once during their closing statement, instead, he continues to jot down notes in his fancy notepad. But when they have finished, when they have had their moment in the spotlight assassinating my character, he rises, straightens his tie and defends me to the hilt.

'Ladies and Gentlemen of the jury, thank you for your time throughout this trial.' Miles begins. 'It has been, I am sure, overwhelming, upsetting and somewhat exhausting. I would like to start by asking you to look across at my client, the most exhausted of us all. You see, my client, Mrs Jade Sawyer, has not known a moment's peace since this trial began. She has been labelled incorrectly on many an occasion now as being manipulative, ruthless, and remorseless. But she is none of those things. Mrs Sawyer has clearly and concisely admitted her guilt in the death of one Mr Jake Walker, an action that she regrets terribly, and an action that was triggered by the violence she suffered over many years at the hands of her husband, and again as she witnessed her lover, Mr Jake Walker, beating her husband to death. It was at this point that Mrs Sawyer was once again left fearing for her own safety.

She has openly spoken of the abuse she suffered at the hands of her husband. Abuse that lasted years, leaving her with a very real diagnosis of PTSD. She has explained in great detail her desperation to flee the man who was harming her, to the point that she was hospitalised after a terrible car accident following her first attempted escape. I would therefore say once more, that my client, Mrs Sawyer, is the most exhausted of us all.

Mrs Sawyer did *not* murder her husband on the day of December 3rd two thousand twenty-five and there is no solid, concrete evidence that she did. This trial has proven that.

I ask you, the jury, to think carefully about your final decision in this tragic case and to sentence my client, Mrs Jade Sawyer on the facts and testimonies that you have before you. The facts clearly show that Mrs Sawyer *is* guilty of the death of Mr Walker, but not that of the murder of her husband Mr Sawyer, of which there is no evidence. No evidence at all.'

As His Honour Judge Rupert Bartholomew-Smythe KC turns to face the jurors, it is at this point that I realise, truly realise, just how much my life is about to change. This is it. This is the moment where everything changes forever and there is nothing I can do to stop it.

'Members of the jury, you have heard all of the testimony concerning this case. It is now up to you to determine the facts. You and you alone are the judges of the fact. In just a moment, the bailiff will take you to the jury room to consider your verdict. Whatever verdict you render must be unanimous, which means that each and every person must agree on the same verdict.'

THE JURY IS OUT ON SAVAGE SAWYER

Whitby News   Thursday 27th August 2026
By: Verity Cobain – News Reporter

A jury has retired to consider whether a trusted Whitby resident is guilty of savagely murdering two men.

Eric Sawyer and Jake Walker were both brutally killed at a remote house in East Keswick in December 2025.
Mrs Jade Sawyer is currently standing trial accused of both of their murders.

Judge Rupert Bartholomew-Smythe KC sent the jury out at Leeds Crown Court to deliberate. A verdict which is eagerly awaited by many.

Prosecutors have said that Mrs Sawyer is devious and sly and a pathological liar. She lacks empathy and feels no remorse whatsoever for the murders of both her husband and her lover.

Mrs Sawyer has admitted to her involvement in the death of her then lover, Jake Walker. But she vehemently denies any involvement in the murder of her husband, Eric Sawyer.

Whitby News will of course keep you all updated on this dreadful crime that has devastated all involved.

Verity Cobain – News Reporter for the Whitby News.

Forty-Three

I can't eat. I can't sleep. I can't function.

It has been twenty-three hours since the jury were sent out to decide my fate. Twenty-three hours of nothingness.

Pauline has driven me crazy with her non-stop split personalities. One minute she agrees that I will only be charged with the murder of Jake. The next, she's cackling away that I'll be joining her in the *lifer club* for double murder. I can't take it. I can't listen to her for a moment longer! The woman is nuts!

Miles has told me that he has done all he can, and even he has no idea which way the jury will swing.

There is nothing left to do now but wait.

Watch the clock, and wait.

Tick Tock…
Tick Tock…
Tick Tock…

Forty-Four

The jurors are out for five days!

Five agonising days!

And now, as I sit here, watching them all take their seats, I want to freeze time. I want to call a halt to proceedings. I want to scream and shout and tell them to wait. I need a moment.

Before they deliver their verdict, I need a moment.

But I can't do that. They're back now and they are ready to condemn me. They are all so eager to get this debacle over and done with, so that they can all go home to their families, back to their lives, away from this horror.

But I just want them to hit pause. Just for a second.

While I was waiting, in my cell, for this moment, I just wanted to know the answer. I just wanted to know what I was facing, so that I could begin to process it. So that I knew exactly how my future looked. But now that the day has finally arrived, now that I am just moments away from the biggest answer to any question ever asked, I am scared.

I don't want to know. Not anymore.

'We the jury find the defendant guilty of the involuntary manslaughter of Mr Jake Walker.'

The silence in the courtroom is deafening as the Judge asks the next question that will alter the course of my life significantly.

'And of the next charge?'

Deathly silence.

I dare not breathe as I watch the juror's lips begin to move.

'We the jury find the defendant *not* guilty of the murder of Mr Eric Sawyer.'

The silence is obliterated...

As boos echo around the courtroom, and I hear my mum sob loudly, the Judge immediately calls for silence.

I don't know how I feel. I need to be alone; I need to process this. They found me not guilty for the murder of Eric, it's all I ever wanted, but now the words have been spoken I don't know how to feel.

The answer to the biggest question has been given.

They've charged me with *involuntary* manslaughter – they don't think I meant to do it!

But I did. At the time, I did.

Is it wrong to feel relieved?

'Mrs Sawyer, if you would please stand.' The Judge begins as I force my shaky legs to move. 'You have today, in a jury of your peers been found guilty of the involuntary manslaughter of one Mr Jake Walker. Whilst there are mitigating circumstances in this offence and subsequent verdict, you have still taken the life of another, and for that, you will be sentenced accordingly. It is therefore my ruling that you will be remanded into custody to serve a sentence of fifteen years imprisonment, of which you will most certainly serve a minimum of seven years.

I hope that you can use this time effectively, not only to rehabilitate yourself, but also to gain the help that you quite evidently need. This court is now adjourned.'

I turn now, to face my family and my friends, to look at them just for a second, it's all I need – but nestled deep amongst their anguish and their pain, I am drawn away as I see only one face staring back at me.

A face that looks happy. Much too happy.

Clara!

IS ABUSED WIFE REALLY TO BLAME FOR VIOLENT MURDERS THAT HAVE SHOCKED WHITBY?

Whitby News   Tuesday 1st September 2026
By: Verity Cobain – News Reporter

A woman who murdered her lover and also helped to dispose of the body of her husband has been sentenced to fifteen years imprisonment, with a possibility of early release after just seven, a sentence that has outraged many.

Jade Sawyer (formerly Locke), of Henrietta Street in Whitby, will serve a minimum of seven years in prison.

The 33-year-old stood by and watched as her lover, Jake Walker beat her husband Eric Sawyer to death with a rock and then coldly planned how they would dispose of his body.
Then in a twisted turn of events, fearing that Mr Walker would in time 'crack and confess', Mrs Swayer savagely attacked him as he showered.

Scenes outside of the court were a mixture of both support and contempt for Mrs Swayer, which leads us to ask the question, 'Was she really to blame?'

Of course, we can never take the law into our own hands, and with no police reports on record pertaining to the alleged suffering that Mrs Sawyer endured, we can only base our response on the witness testimonies of her friends, but does that mean to say that she was lying? How well can we ever know what happens behind closed doors?

We do however know that Mr Sawyer had been accused of violence and abuse previously, a case that never made it to court, and so we ask again, if this man had a record of violence, was Mrs Sawyer really to blame for defending herself?

If Mrs Sawyer is to be believed, she, by her own admission did not report these crimes, she did not tell her family, she suffered alone, as many wives and husbands do in these situations. Is it fair to say then that she just snapped, or so desperate was she to have her life back she was thrust into a situation that she could not see a way out of? A situation that very quickly escalated out of control.

We can never fully comprehend the inner workings of a person's mind, and I doubt that we will ever fully understand what Mrs Sawyer was thinking at the time of these murders, but with a minimum of seven years in prison, she has plenty of time on which to ponder this.

Verity Cobain – News Reporter for the Whitby News.

Forty-Five

Seven years!

It could have been worse.

I could have been charged with the murder of Eric and that would have carried a hefty sentence for sure. As it is involuntary manslaughter was the best I was going to get and I hadn't even predicted that. I had thought they would come out with full-blown manslaughter for Jake and 100% murder for Eric.

So it's a relief really.

Now all I have to do is survive the next seven years!

I've had a lot of time to think since my sentencing, and the one question that plays heavy on my mind is, would I do it all again? If I were faced with the same life, and the same people, would I act any differently? Would I change anything?

The answer... is I don't know.

I think I did what I had to do to survive. I know that I made some dumb choices along the way – being hit by a car is a particular favourite of mine. Not to mention filming dead bodies in a well. They weren't the best decisions I could have made, and I suppose I would change those if I could.

The thing is, people say, '*Why didn't you just leave?*' – well, because it's not that easy when you're present in that situation. It sounds like it should be, but it isn't. When you are there, the violence, the hatred, the abuse, the mind games, it's magnified a thousand times. They manipulate the way you think, they break you down until you can't think.

It sounds like it's easy to leave from the outside.

But it isn't.

It wasn't.

The prosecution barrister was right about one thing though, I'm not a victim. I'm a survivor.

Pauline has been a nightmare since I returned. She was hoping that I'd get a longer sentence, so we could be roomies forever, so she's plenty pissed that I only got seven years. I say only. It might as well be forever. But, I wanted to be punished for Jake's death, I needed to be. So I need to suck it up and get on with it.

I've managed to swap jobs and I'm now far away from the dirty kitchen and the dirty underpants. I've managed to land myself a cushy little number in the prison library. It's not as elaborate as it sounds. It's a small room with half a dozen bookshelves and a tiny table, but I like it in there, it's peaceful.

The next seven years are going to be tough. Of course they are, it's a prison, so I need to savour the small things. I'm planning on learning something while I'm here, counselling maybe so that I can put it towards a useful job when I'm released. I doubt very much Mr. Timmons will have me back now, which is a shame because I enjoyed that little job. But, really? A murderer working the tills? And then there's Clara.

It was clear to me the moment I saw her in that courtroom grinning like a cheshire cat that she was the letter writer. I said it, didn't I, it's always the quiet ones.

I can't let Clara get away with what she's done to me. Sure, I would probably have been caught eventually, but she caused me no end of terror with those letters. She was the one that brought everything to a head. I would have had longer with my family had she not done what she did. She must know from the papers what I went through, what I had to fight to survive, and yet she still smiled at me, victorious.

She has no idea what being terrified feels like and I hope she never does.

Dear Jade,

I wanted to write and say thank you.

It's probably wrong of me to be grateful that you were brave enough to do what I could not, but I am. I am grateful, I am thankful, I am for the first time in a long time, happy. I feel like I can finally breathe.

I know that you must have conflicting feelings. You've suffered in ways that not many people could even imagine in their worst nightmares, and still, even after all of that, you must now face further years of loss. But you can do this Jade! You have faced worse; you have conquered worse – you are stronger than I will ever be.

I am proud of us Jade. I am proud of you.

In seven years you can walk out of that place knowing that you not only saved yourself, but you saved me and countless other women that may have fallen for his superficial charm.

If it's okay I'd like to continue writing to you. Maybe even visit? It's okay if you don't want that though, if it's too much of a reminder. I will understand.

Stay strong, you've got this.
Amber xx

Forty-Six

'Stella? I didn't expect to see you ever again.' I exclaim, shocked at her sudden appearance in the visitor's room. 'What are you doing here?'

'I didn't like the way we left things the last time we saw one another, and well, I thought maybe we could pick up where we left off?'

'Why?'

'Because I want to help you?'

'Are you asking me if that's what you want to do?'

'Well, I…'

She looks nervous, and on edge, which is hardly surprising considering where we are, but something seems off. She wasn't exactly shaking pom poms of support during my trial, so this is all just a bit, odd.

'Why are you really here, Stella?'

'Okay.' She takes a deep breath, 'the thing is, I've not really had many interesting clients walk through my door, and well, you, you're the most interesting one I can think of, so I thought maybe I might write…'

'A book?' I laugh. 'Were you going to say write a book?

Why is everybody suddenly writing books?! No, Stella, that's not going to happen, not ever.'

'If you just hear me out…'

'I've heard enough, thanks. Look, it was great to see you, really, but…'

'Jade, please, I just thought…'

'I'm sorry Stella. I'm sorry that I picked your offices to come and offload in, I really am, but the thing is, you weren't really that helpful. You just asked stupid questions, gave me idiotic homework and then bailed on me when I needed you. I don't want to help you write a book; I don't want to help you do anything. I just want to do my time, not get shanked and then go home. Is that really too much to ask?'

'Right.' She pouts. 'I guess that's that then. I won't take up any more of your time.'

'I know you're going to write it anyway Stella. I hope you make lots of money off of the back of this misery.'

As she turns to walk away from me, I feel suddenly deflated. Is this all I'm going to get now? Requests for interviews and letters from crazy fans of the macabre? People dissecting my life so that they can write a stupid book? If that's how it's going to be while I'm inside, then god only knows what it will be like when I'm on the outside. But then, I have seven years to go until I have to worry about that I suppose.

Verity Cobain wrote to me a little while ago also. I threw her letter straight in the bin. She was another one who wanted to do an in-depth interview with me. She's like a vulture that one, and I have a feeling I'll have to avoid her like the plague when I'm released.

You know, this whole thing has put me right off murder documentaries. Funny that.

As night draws in, I return to my cell with a heavy heart. I can't quite comprehend all that has happened to me. I'm nobody, just a shop assistant from a seaside town. What did I do to deserve all of this?

Why was Eric even drawn to me?

Could he sense that I was weak? Vulnerable? Sad? Or would any woman have done, so long as he could beat her into submission?

You could come from any background, lower class, middle class, stinking rich and still have this happen to you. It would seem that abusers aren't really that picky.

Now, I'm not saying that everyone will end up dumping two dead bodies into a well, or something equally as peculiar – but you never know. You really don't.

Everyone in this prison has made a terrible decision that has led them here. Some of course don't care and are proud of what they've done. But the rest? The ones that cry at night? – They regret it.

Why don't I cry at night if I regret it?

Because I can't. I've cried too many tears already. I don't have any left. I know that prison is going to change me, make me a little harder and a little tougher to crack, and maybe that's not a bad thing. Maybe I could do with toughening up.

I don't want to be too different though. I actually like Jade Locke. She's still in here somewhere, I know she is, and one day, hopefully soon, I will find her again.

That girl who dances all night and drinks like a fish and sings really badly at karaoke and wears red lipstick and falls asleep in her Halloween costume. She is in here.

I know she is.

Jade,

I know that you saw me in the courtroom. I was hardly difficult to miss was I, as I was the only one who was truly happy to see you sentenced. You must be wondering why I wrote to you before, why I tormented you as I did. It's simple really. You took Jake from me. First by flirting with him and then by killing him.

I followed you that night. I saw what you did to Eric, the fight, how you made Jake feel like he had to kill him for you. And then I watched as you forced him to hide the body. I don't know what happened in the house between you and Jake, only that the next time I saw him he was dead. You killed him. You murdered the man that I loved! I was going to call the police there and then, but I was interested to see what you would do next. God, you were pathetic. Crying and cleaning, crying and cleaning. I should have called the police just to end the dullness of it all.

Then you went home, as though nothing had happened. As though the blood of two men were not on your hands. Partying, drinking, shopping – what a joke! You were alive while my Jake was dead!

I knew then that you had to suffer the way that I was suffering.

It was a hoot though when you and that idiotic friend of yours turned up in Bardsey, all scared and pathetic. It was so difficult for me not to laugh out loud as you bumbled your way through trying to work out who it was.

I'm glad that you're in prison Jade. I hope you rot like you left my poor Jake to rot.

I don't think seven years is long enough, but it will have to do. For now.

C.

Forty-Seven

Thrusting the letter into Heidi's hands I sit down heavily and put my head on the table.

'What is this?'

'It's from Clara. Read it.' I urge, 'especially that last bit.'

'Christ, she really is batshit crazy!' She gasps as her eyes quickly scan the pages. 'Has this just arrived?'

'Yesterday. You see the last part though – '*but it will have to do. For now.*' What the hell does that mean?'

'It means she's a total loser with nothing better to do with her time. Just bin it and ignore her.'

'It's a threat, Heids! She blames me for taking her love away, she wants revenge, and *this.*' I wave my arms dramatically around me, 'clearly isn't enough.'

'Well, I mean, you kinda did.' She smiles.

'Not helpful Heidi, at all!'

'Sorry. You're right. Do you want me to go and have a word with her? Find out what her deal is?'

'No! God no! I don't want you anywhere near her, she's unstable. Just keep a lookout, okay. Anything weird or suspicious then call the police, but please don't confront her. There's no telling what she's capable of.'

'Do you honestly think she'd try to harm you? She's got a bloody long wait if that's her plan.'

'All the longer for her to stew on it.'

'Or, turning that frown upside down, all the longer for her to get the hell over it.'

'What if she doesn't want to hurt me? What if she wants to hurt someone I care about, like I did to her?'

'Okay, you're being a little irrational right now. She is not going to risk ending up in here with you just for a little payback, is she?'

'It isn't little though is it – I murdered the love of her life!'

'On an *involuntary* basis.' Heidi adds with a wink. 'Well, you never know who's listening!'

'What am I going to do?'

'Nothing. One, because you're in here where she can't get you, and two, because I will keep a lookout for any suspicious stuff happening. She'd be daft to try anything, Jade.'

'She's mental Heids. Mental people don't do normal things.'

'You're normal and look where it got you.'

'Thanks.'

'I'm joking, I'll speak to Gordon, Jess and Nicky, to make

them aware and I'll keep an eye on your mum and dad. Will that make you feel better?'

'Yes.' I smile, weakly, 'and thank you. I would really appreciate that.'

'Don't let her do this to you. She's annoyed now but it will soon wear off. She'll get bored and move on. Honestly, that girl doesn't look like she has much staying power for anything, never mind a vendetta.'

'Have you seen much of Ben? What if they're in it together?'

'I highly doubt Ben gives a shit about anything other than his beer and his darts. He came after you because Eric wasn't there to stop him. I've not seen him, but that can only be a good thing because people move on – it's natural.'

'There's nothing natural about *him*.' I scowl.

'No, that's true. But he also has a brain the size of a hamster turd, so he's not a threat. Honestly.'

'I murdered her true love, Heidi.'

'You probably did him a favour. Oh, don't look at me like that. Would you want to be adored by her? Little Miss Bunny Boiler? No? Didn't think so. Throw the letter away. You have nothing to worry about from her.'

Back in my cell, I think about everything that Heidi said. Maybe Clara will get over it. Maybe I don't have anything to fear from her now. Surely I've suffered the worst that life can throw at me – what's a few words on a page?

I am sorry that I killed the man she loved, and if it were me who had lost somebody that I cared deeply for at the hands of another, then I'm sure I would react the same way. No sentence would be long enough. So doesn't it stand to reason then that sweet little Clara might just want more from me? Is it reasonable to assume that she will wait for me to get out and then try and destroy everything that I have? Will she try and take my love from me?

What would I do if I were her?

I know only one thing for certain as I start this rather lengthy prison sentence, I will not allow anyone to take away my freedom ever again. All I've ever wanted since this fiasco started was to go home, and nobody is going to take that away from me.

There is after all more room in the well now.

I know, I know, I shouldn't jest. The past seven years have literally been hell on earth.

I have doubted my own self, doubted my inner strength and doubted my own worth.

I have stood, bloody and beaten, I have taken each hit with

a steely grit that I did not know I possessed.

I have endured and I have survived.

　　I am not a victim.

I am a fighter. A champion. My own hero.

I know that I should not jest. I know that it's inappropriate. I know that it's no laughing matter. But as Heidi said so many months ago, '*We have to laugh sometimes Jade, because this situation is getting way darker than either of us anticipated.*' Well, she was right. I do need to laugh and I do need to smile. And that darkness? That's over with now. The worst of the darkest days are over.

I'm walking towards the light. I'm finally free.

… Sort of!

Acknowledgements

I would like to first, as always thank my husband, Paul. You've listened to me plot and scheme, helped me when it sounded bonkers and offered ideas and suggestions. You've hated Eric *bloody* Sawyer just as I have, every step of the way. You've driven me to Whitby again for more inspiration and we've scoffed the best fish and chips ever – again!

Thank you to Kat at Pink Lady Books for all of your support.

Thank you to my wonderful readers, you are the best. I love your feedback and I thank you for taking the time to read what I write and for your lovely reviews. I appreciate you all more than you will ever know.

I would also like to extend my heartfelt appreciation and thanks to Craig Whitfield. I am extremely grateful for the time and effort that you have dedicated to meticulously reviewing and refining this book. Your keen attention to detail and insightful suggestions have made a significant impact on this story, and for that, I thank you.

Whitby, you have, as always, been fabulous!

Please read on for a short snippet of the final instalment of Jade's story; NOW IS ALL WE HAVE

Dear Reader

Thank you for reading NOW YOU DON'T.

I hope that you enjoyed sharing the continuation of Jade's journey with me.

I know that there are many other books that you could have picked to read and I am extremely grateful that you selected mine.

I would love to hear from you, and if you would be kind enough to leave me a review on Amazon it would really make my day.

All feedback is greatly appreciated.

Thank you again for taking the time to read my book.

www.emmalbealauthor.com

Facebook: Emma L Beal

BOOK CLUB QUESTIONS

Which character did you most relate to and why?

What scene resonated with you most on a personal level? (Why? How did it make you feel?)

Did any part of this book strike a particular emotion in you? Which part and what emotion did the book make you feel?

How would you adapt this book into a TV show?
Who would you cast in the leading roles?

If you got the chance to ask the author of this book one question, what would it be?

If you could hear this same story from another person's point of view, who would you choose?

What do you think will happen next to the main characters?

COMING SOON

PART 3

(the finale)

NOW IS ALL WE HAVE

**Whitby, North Yorkshire – idyllic, peaceful, picturesque,
Where home truly is where the heart is.**

A kiss put on hold.
A family shattered.
A secret so deadly it would not be silenced.
What would it take to finally break her?

As her seven-year prison sentence comes to an end, Jade Locke knows
that this is her chance to finally turn her misfortune around. Gordon,
her not so secret love has big plans, her best friend Heidi wants to drink
and dance, and all Jade wants to do is paddle in the sea and eat fish and
chips. But will the townsfolk of Whitby welcome her home,
or will she be shunned?

Home is all she's ever wanted.
And she will get what she wants, no matter the cost.

Sneak Preview

NOW IS ALL WE HAVE

One

The thing about prison is, you have a lot of time to think. All of those conversations where you wish you'd said this, or said that... you can play those on repeat all day long.

Honestly, it never loses its shine.

The thing about prison is, you have a lot of time on your hands, and not an awful lot to fill it.

I spent the majority of my time inside avoiding confrontation and prison politics, and I was successful... mostly.

No, I didn't look at you funny.

No, I never said anything.

No, I don't want to fight you. Jesus, why would I?

There were times of course when talking my way out of a *situation* just didn't work – and inevitably a fight would break out, a fight that I lost every single time. But mostly, I spent my time thinking.

Because you see, the thing about prison is, you have an awful lot of time to think about those people that did you wrong. And then you think some more. And some more.

I killed Jake, we all know that. I didn't kill Eric though. But then I didn't do anything to stop it either.

I deserved my seven years; I deserved it being tough. I probably deserved longer, though I'll never admit that. *Involuntary manslaughter.* It still puzzles me how they came to that conclusion.

Was it the PTSD diagnosis?

Was it Miles's clever courtroom tactics?

Was it the fact that against all odds they truly believed me when I told them about Eric?

Was it the fact that Amber's testimony backed me up?

Whatever it was, they were wrong. I did mean to kill Jake. There was nothing *involuntary* about it, and that is something that I will take to the grave with me. That is one secret I will never share.

Prison has been tough. I didn't expect a walk in the park. I didn't expect an easy ride. But I also didn't expect seven long years of watching my back, every minute of every day. Of course, things weren't made any easier by the fact that my cellmate, crazy Pauline decided to top herself. I did not see that one coming!

They gave me a new cellmate of course, Veronica, and she was even more bonkers than Pauline, if you can believe that! Veronica would talk over and over to her baby – the baby that not five weeks prior she had shoved in the oven like a Christmas turkey– so yeah, that was great.

Prison has been a barrel of laughs. Not.
Gordon true to his word finally plucked up the courage to visit me and actually came every week, which was great. Sometimes my mum would come with him, or one of the girls, but never dad. Dad just couldn't face it. I can't say I blame him. Prison sucks.

Even Amber has been to see me. She hated it, I could tell. Not the seeing me, I don't think, but the place. The depressing walls and groans of despair, so I gave her an out. Said it would be easier for me if we just wrote – she knew I was lying, but she was relieved.

I had lots of requests for interviews, which I politely declined. At that point, I felt like enough of my life had been dragged through the tabloids, and eventually, they all just stopped asking.

I am glad that I admitted my guilt over Jake's death, despite how hard this has been, because at least I know that I can go home without that hanging over my head. I know that I've done my time, I've served my sentence, I've been suitably punished. But, there are a lot of people out there who don't think that seven years was long enough, and Clara is one of those people.

I know it sounds a little bit obsessive. I should just move on, forget about her. But I can't. And actually, I doubt very much that she has forgotten about me. God only knows what she has planned for when I'm home.

I do feel bad. She loved Jake – but I didn't know that. I wouldn't have stepped on her toes if I'd known that. But I don't believe I deserved the torment of her letters because she wasn't brave enough to declare her feelings for him. She heard all about Eric, she knew what I'd been through, and still, she mocked me.

I want to forget about Clara. I want to go home and paddle in the sea, eat fish and chips, sing karaoke and dance the night away – but something tells me that isn't going to be how my story ends. Something tells me I have more to worry about than I can possibly imagine.

NOW IS ALL WE HAVE

COMING SOON

FOLLOW ME ON FACEBOOK

'Emma L Beal'

FOR MORE BOOK UPDATES

Printed in Great Britain
by Amazon